Autumn Winifred Oliver Does Things Different

Autumn Winifred Oliver
Does Things Different

Kristin O'Donnell Tubb

delacorte press

Published by Delacorte Press
an imprint of Random House Children's Books
a division of Random House, Inc.
New York

This is a work of fiction. All incidents and dialogue, and all
characters with the exception of some well-known historical and public figures,
are products of the author's imagination and are not to be construed as real.
Where real-life historical or public figures appear, the situations, incidents, and
dialogues concerning those persons are fictional and are not intended to depict
actual events or to change the fictional nature of the work. In all other respects,
any resemblance to persons living or dead is entirely coincidental.

Delacorte Press and colophon are registered
trademarks of Random House, Inc.

Visit us on the Web! www.randomhouse.com/kids

Educators and librarians, for a variety of teaching tools, visit us at
www.randomhouse.com/teachers

Library of Congress Cataloging-in-Publication Data
Tubb, Kristin O'Donnell.
Autumn Winifred Oliver does things different / Kristin O'Donnell Tubb. — 1st ed.
p. cm.
Summary: Autumn Winifred Oliver, an eleven-year-old girl living in Cades
Cove, Eastern Tennessee, during the Depression, watches her grandfather as he
tries to persuade his neighbors to back the proposed Great Smoky Mountains
National Park, but when they discover that the government representative is
lying to them, Gramps becomes even more resourceful. Includes author's note
about the history of the park. Includes bibliographical references.
ISBN: 978-0-385-73569-8 (hardcover) — ISBN: 978-0-385-90558-9
(Gibraltar lib. bdg.)
[1. Grandfathers—Fiction. 2. Depressions—1929—Fiction. 3. Country life—
Tennessee—Fiction. 4. Great Smoky Mountains National Park (N.C. and
Tenn.)—Fiction. 5. Tennessee—History—20th Century—Fiction.]
PZ7.T796Au 2008
[Fic]—dc22
2007037411

The text of this book is set in 12-point Goudy.

Book design by Kenny Holcomb

Printed in the United States of America

10 9 8 7 6 5 4 3 2 1

First Edition

Acknowledgments

There are a few people whose life's work helped make this story possible. Durwood Dunn, a professor at Tennessee Wesleyan College, was born and raised in Cades Cove, and he has shared his rich history through several books. Much of the flavor of Cades Cove captured in this story is thanks to the detailed accounts of life in the Cove recorded by Dr. Dunn. Also vitally important to the spirit of this text is the work of Veta Wilson King. Ms. King, a feature writer for the *Mountain Press*, a newspaper in Sevier County, Tennessee, has the gift of drawing stories out of people and the foresight to record them for future generations. Thank you, too, to Randy Russell and Janet Barnett, who have preserved many of the ghost stories popular in east Tennessee. A. Randolph Shields and Carlos C. Campbell are both Great Smoky Mountains National Park historians whose work I cherish.

My thanks to the members of the CAPS critique group: Kathy Rhodes, Susie Dunham, Colleen Speroff, Currie Powers, and Chance Chambers.

They were the first to lay eyes on Autumn, and she's stronger for it. Thank you, too, to the numerous members of the Midsouth chapter of the Society of Children's Book Writers and Illustrators, who offered suggestions on this story. Special thanks to Shirley Amitrano and Linda Ragsdale, perhaps the two best critiquers on the planet. Hugs to you both!

My gratitude to Kathryn Knight, friend and mentor, who opened the door to children's publishing for me. And to Wendy Loggia, my editor, who took Autumn by the hand and gently led her toward better, smarter choices: many, many thanks! Autumn's a hard one to rein in, and you did it masterfully.

Big hugs to the members of the St. Paul's Playgroup, especially Tina Cahalan Jones, who helped with many of the behind-the-scenes aspects of this book.

I'm blessed to have a mother-in-law, Theresa Tubb, who understood my dream and who volunteered her babysitting/grandmotherly services to help me achieve it. My parents, Jack and Helen O'Donnell, told me I could do anything I want to do, and then gave me every opportunity to do it. I love you both. And to my beautiful kiddos, Chloe and Jack: thank you for believing in "someday." You are deeply loved.

For Byron.
Love!

1

I do things different.
It helps to remind
yourself of that
when you're attending
your own funeral.

So there I stood, on something akin to a big, bald behind. Mighty appropriate circumstances, considering what came next.

I was in the Meadow in the Sky on top of
Thunderhead Mountain. Thunderhead gets its name
because it's so high up, thunderstorms crack and
boom and dump rain *below* you. There aren't any
trees up there, so the mountaintop is nothing but a
big, swishy meadow. Folks around here call it a
"bald," and it looks enough like a hairless head. But
all those mountains together, they look more to me
like they're baring their rumps to the heavens above.

So I figure all this talk about a national park is nothing but a bunch of hoo-ha. Who'd travel across the country to see *this*?

Truth be told, I cotton to the balds, myself. Those balds, they're a bit of a mystery. Nobody knows for sure why trees don't grow on them. It's not that the mountains are too tall, or that the weather is too cold. I suppose those balds just don't want to be like every other mountain.

Yeah, I guess I'll miss old Thunderhead most of all once we finally join Pop in Knoxville. *Knoxville*. I glow like a lightning bug every time I think about all that big-city living. Just nineteen more days.

Knoxville's thirty miles away as the crow flies, but boy, are those some bumpy miles by land. There's but one road out of Cades Cove, and it's snowed in three months of the year. Cades Cove is like an island, a speck of a town surrounded by wave after wave of mountains. (Course, I've never seen the ocean. I hear it's salty. Me, I prefer sweets.) Those mountains circling our tiny town serve to keep out all that's new. Others in the Cove are just fine with the old, but me, I like new.

Don't get me wrong—for the most part, I love this here Cove. But I'm not cut from the same chunk of wood as the folks who've whittled away their lives here. I reckon I'm a chain saw in a stack of axes. See, Autumn Winifred Oliver does things different. Least that's what our neighbors are fond of saying. Course, they don't use that exact word, "different." They're more apt to say "rascally" or "rampageous" or "up to no good."

Another storm stirred below. My dusty blond hair whipped across my face, stinging it like a sunburn. I smelled the drops in the air. The pine trees way below bent practically in half in all the frenzy. It'd make a right nice drawing if I were inclined to sit and sketch. But, wind aside, the weather up on Thunderhead was clear as glass. When it's clear, it feels like you can reach right up and touch the sun, and that's what I was aiming to do. So I'm surprised I heard the bells at all.

Church bells ringing on any day other than the Sabbath is a sound that prickles your neck hairs. On those days, ringing bells tally up the age of the Cove's latest dearly departed. Most times, just counting the number of tolls tells you who's passed. So I listened hard and counted: *ding, dong, ding, dong, ding, dong, ding, dong, ding, dong, ding.*

Eleven tolls total. *Wait . . . eleven? That ain't*

right! I did some quick figuring: me, Donnie Dunlap, and Twig Ogle hit the mark. But Donnie'd been in the Sugarlands all summer helping his uncle, and Twig and her family were on their fancy vacation to Gatlinburg that week. So time being, I was the only one in the whole dang Cove who was eleven! But the bells stopped ringing right at that number, no joshing.

So that's pretty much how I found out I'd died.

Now, it doesn't take a cartful of clever and cunning to know that had I *really* died, I wouldn't be here to tell this story. But I'd never passed on before, so I bit myself between my thumb and forefinger just to make certain. Nope—definitely still (ouch!) here. Yet after I found out what happened, I'd *like* to have died.

I scrambled home quicker than spit on a griddle to see what my death was all about. I'd just slid down a muddy slope into our backyard when my eyes locked with big fat Aunt Lydia, my mama's cousin. There she was, all puffy and puckered and fanning herself because she'd apparently run over from her farm when she heard the tolls, too. As soon as she laid those beady little black eyes of hers on me, the walking dead, her lips formed a tiny pink O and she passed out cold. And God has a sense of humor, as Mama likes to say, because right then the sky broke open and buckets of rain dumped on us both.

I do things different. It helps to remind yourself of that when you're dragging one of your heftiest kin through the mud.

I heaved and hauled and pushed big ole Aunt Lydia into the dogtrot so's she'd stay dry. And let me tell you, I might be small for my age, but I'm scrappy. I hefted that sack of potatoes onto that porch and I left her there. I figured I'd suffer my punishments for seeing her knickers later on (as if *seeing* her knickers wasn't punishment enough).

"Mama!" I yelled into the kitchen, then into the parlor. "Mama?"

There was a small crowd inside. Mo Jackson and his son, Beef, were there. So were Uncle John and Uncle John Too and Uncle Mack. Katie and Mama and Aunt Patsy and Mrs. Tillman were all packed in as well. They huddled over the davenport, where my gramps lay sputtering and coughing like a cat working up one heckuva hairball. Mama was all teary.

"It's a miracle!" she muttered, dabbing her moist eyes with the corner of her apron. The neighbors nodded with hung-open jaws. "It's a miracle!"

"*What's* a miracle?" I asked, pushing my way up to the front of the crowd. After all, those bells had just rung up my death. Wasn't this my funeral? Shouldn't I have a good view of the goings-on?

Gramps pulled himself up on one of his shriveled old elbows. His milky eyes finally focused on the crowd above him, and his face twisted into deep ruts like those you see in the creek beds when it hasn't rained in weeks. He grunted.

"What the hell are you lookin' at?"

He did—he said it! He said the *h*-word outside of church, right there in front of all those ladies. Now, if that room hadn't been silent before, he hushed us all up with that little gem. And at this point, more and more rain-soaked folks had crowded into our tiny parlor, on account of those bells announcing my death and all. So practically half the Cove heard my gramps rip that one out. Jeez!

Finally, a soaking wet Paul Peterson stepped forward, grabbed my knobby elbow, and shook me a little, almost to test if I was really there. He looked down at me, then over at my wheezing gramps, then at my mother.

"Martha," he said. "Exactly who here is dead?"

Mama blinked once, twice, three times, as if she was looking into the sun rather than at this soggy crowd of neighbors.

"Why, Daddy, of course," she said, turning to Gramps on the couch. "At least, he was. Fell from the loft of Jackson's barn. We were just about to put the pennies over his eyes"—at this, the crowd sucked in their breaths—"when he started wheezing. It's a miracle, I tell ya! A miracle!" Mama rapped her knuckles on the wooden table beside her to keep future miracles from passing by our house altogether.

"I should've never burned that sassafras wood last week," she said, shaking her head. A couple of folks in the crowd clicked their tongues—sassafras wood burned *indoors*? Well, no wonder!

Then Mama cocked her head like our old porch dog, Jeb, and a frazzled lock of brown hair loosed itself from her bun. "Who else would it be?"

I stepped forward. "Mama," I whispered. Suddenly

I felt itchy in my skin after the news of my death had rung through the Cove and echoed off the mountains. "The bell rang eleven times."

Now, I reckon that normally, on a day when the bell at the Missionary Baptist Church had just toted up the age of her youngest baby girl, Mama'd be a slobbering, blubbery mess. At least, I like to imagine that. But today, instead of fainting cold dead on the spot like big fat Aunt Lydia, Mama just whistled. Whistled!

"Looks like we've dodged that old Grim Reaper twice today. We are truly blessed."

"But Mama," my voice squeaked. "Why *eleven?*"

" 'Twas a mistake, Winnie," she said, and ruffled my tangled hair. (She's the only one who can call me Winnie without suffering a black-and-blue shin afterwards. Not to mention the hair-ruffling thing.) "I sent Joe Jackson to the church to ring it fifty-three times for Daddy. Just after he left, the wheezing begun. Somebody must've sent word to stop the ringing. Funny how they stopped right on your number, huh, Win?" She was all smiles.

"Funny? It's thumbing my nose at fate, more likely! Now I'm jinxed for sure!" There. I'd said it. I knew by the faces of our neighbors, who were still crowding into our parlor one by one, that they thought so, too. *There goes Autumn Oliver,* they'd say later. *She's supposed to be dead.*

Me, a walking ghost? Now, *that's* different.

Gramps silenced the crowd with a grunt, which just goes to show you how bad off he must've been, to stay quiet as long as he did. "This is all well and good, folks, but show's over. I got work to do." He groaned his way to his feet and quickly hunched over, placing his hands on his knees to steady himself. I'd never seen Gramps look so weak.

Mama cleared her throat, adjusted her apron, and turned to me and Katie. "That does it. Girls, we're moving in with your gramps."

"What?" I shrieked in unison with Katie. Normally, me and my big sis don't think enough alike to shriek anything in unison. But *this*! Death suddenly didn't look so bad.

"No Knoxville?" Katie asked, clamping her arms across her broad chest. She shook her head, flinging tight brown pincurls around her face.

"But we gotta go to Knoxville!" I shouted. "What about Pop? He's been there long enough without us girls."

"Yeah! Autumn's right," Katie said. I squinched

my eyes at her to see if she was being sassy, but it looked like my sister actually agreed with me. That's a first.

Mama chewed on the inside of her lip, and I thought we had her. Mama couldn't leave Pop alone! If I knew anything at all, I knew how much my parents loved each other. Salt and pepper, they were. Everyone said so. Tears pooled in Mama's soft brown eyes, and she swiped at one with a raw, red knuckle. "He'll just have to wait awhile longer, I suppose. Kin is kin. Your gramps needs us."

No Knoxville!

No movie theaters.

No soda counters.

No clear-as-a-bell radio play.

No Pop.

Mama had cried for two days solid when Pop first sprang the idea of moving to Knoxville a few months ago. Katie and I had danced in circles—we were moving to a real *city*, with drugstores and train tracks and strangers! But Mama'd said she'd never live in that durn city and that Pop must be out of his blasted mind. I'd never heard Mama talk so salty.

"Kin is kin," Mama now repeated in a whisper, and her face softened. "We'll just have a little delay, is all." It occurred to me just how grim Mama had grown over the past few weeks: her plump features had pulled taut, and her round brown eyes had narrowed into a squint. But now that she had an excuse to stay in the Cove, she appeared to melt like butter before our eyes. She *said* we were staying to take care of Gramps, but I knew we were really staying because Mama was scareder than a possum in daylight to live in a city as big and noisy and dangerous as Knoxville. But I'd had no idea Mama would move in with her father just to stay in the Cove. She was either mighty concerned about him or mighty scared of that slice of heaven.

Tilly McBroom stepped forward and scooped out the plug of tobacco resting between her gum and front lip.

"Tom," she croaked at Gramps, "don't make these girls give up movin' to the big city. You gots a house. I gots furniture. What say you?"

Two or three giggles got loose from the crowd, but I could feel the jealousy of the other old biddies crackle in the air. I knew what they were thinking: *Why didn't I think to propose?* Gramps was quite the catch, as he was the only widower over forty in the whole Cove. And he'd likely be rich soon, what with all the work he'd done on this national park. Good.

Let 'em fight over him. Better *they* end up with him than me.

"There!" Katie spun toward Mama, and parts of her plump frame spun farther than others. "Gramps'll get married. Done. Now can we move to Knoxville?"

Gramps unfolded from his hunch to his full six-foot-plus height and hooked his thumbs through his overall straps. "Thank you for the offer, Miz Tilly, but I think I'll pass. And Martha, I surely don't want you and your two leeches comin' over and stealin' all my food."

"Leeches!" Katie shrilled. Her green eyes flared, and those shiny curls of hers hopped around her head like wet frogs. "No suitor will come knocking at my door if we're at *that* place!"

"Can't we at least move him in here?" I waved my hand around our tiny parlor. "Our house is so much bigger than his . . . his . . ." I couldn't bring myself to say the word.

"Winnie, this house is sold, remember?" Mama reminded me.

"Quicker than a snap, this house went," Tilly McBroom said, and snapped, as if to underline her point.

"Sight unseen," Uncle John Too added.

It had been the talk of the Cove for weeks—how fast our house had sold once we decided to move. Whoever bought it must be rich or crazy or both. They'd never laid eyes on the place, and they up and paid cash money for the thing. Mama says it's because her house is full of clean living. Everyone else says it's someone going to turn this box into a hotel when the park opens. Fine by me, long as I'm in Knoxville.

But I'm *not* in Knoxville, and it's looking like I won't be anytime soon.

Mama patted Gramps's arm. "We'll be in by the end of the week, Daddy."

That happy, glowy lightning bug that once was Autumn Winifred Oliver? Squashed flat and fizzled out.

2

**I do things different.
It helps to remind
yourself of that
when you're doing
your kin's dirty work.**

Gramps's house was just eleven miles away on the other side of the Cove, but it felt like the other side of the moon. It was off the main road, down a winding dust trail, through a tangled mess of trees, over a swinging suspension bridge that groaned under the weight of a toad, and across a trickle of muddy creek. There sat his drafty, dirty old cabin.

Cabin! There—I said it. *Cabin.* Gramps didn't have a modern frame house like most folks in the Cove. His home was made of huge chiseled logs, worn as smooth as smoky glass over the years. The only thing stopping the wind from blowing right through the chinks in the wood were the layers of rotting newspaper that someone had crammed into the holes long ago.

Gramps was right proud of this heap of logs, he was. Said it was built by his grandparents, one of the first houses in the Cove. When he'd told us that, Katie'd run her finger across a windowpane and lifted off a generous lot of dust. "I can tell," she'd huffed.

We moved in two days after Gramps's little brush with death. Mom and Katie and I all shared a room, one little spot that was likely meant to store food instead of serve as a bedroom. This was nothing like the house we'd left across the Cove, where Katie and I had each had our own room upstairs. And in Knoxville, a huge house sat waiting for us, a house that even had a front porch and closets. And here we sat in this dump. It was hard to imagine Mama growing up here. She's tidier than a hummingbird, and this place was a rubbish heap. Mama said things had been different when Granny was alive. My granny must've been some kind of miracle worker.

"But a sixteen-year-old needs her privacy!" Katie whined when she saw our living quarters.

Mama let loose one of her deep sighs. "Whatever

you can do before the eyes of the Lord you can do in front of us, Katie."

And so we bunked up together. Between Mama's knitting supplies and Katie's perfume bottles and fake jewels, there was hardly any room at all for my art stuff. Mama could nest into any little nook, but Katie and I'd never shared a room before. Can't say I recall us having shared anything before. Unless you count the hand-me-downs I'm forced to wear: three sizes too big and ten times too frilly. Katie's roomy clothes hang on my scrawny frame like a horse blanket on a hound dog.

"Okay, so let's make the best of this," Katie grumbled. She drummed her thick fingers on the chest of drawers. "I'm willing to go splitsies on my toilet water, my talcum powder, and my Camay soap while we're stuck in this hole." Katie pointed at three fancy packages as she said this. "But anything to the *left* of my strand of pearls is for-bidden. *For-bidden*. Got it?" I glanced at the shiny bottles and containers and realized I didn't even know what cold cream did or how witch hazel might make you prettier.

"Can I borrow your books?" I asked. Katie had more books than our schoolhouse, and huge stacks now teetered in every corner of our tiny new room.

She tugged her earlobe while she considered that one. "Yeah, but don't dog-ear the pages, you hear? Use a bookmark like a civilized human being for once. Now, let's divvy up your stuff. Those paintbrushes of yours just might make do as makeup brushes. . . ."

But the worst part? No running water! I'm not joshing—we had to go into the backyard and pump our bathwater by hand. I might not have minded so much, but the wailing from Katie was near unbearable.

"It's 1934, for heaven's sake!" she said, slinging her wrist at the water pump. "Everyone should have running water, no excuses. And an *outhouse*? Really, no one should have to endure an outdoor privy.

"Tell you what, Autumn," she said, eyeballing the water pump and tugging that earlobe again. I never could tell if one of Katie's earlobe tugs would leave me with the short end of the stick or if it signaled a true give-and-take. "I'll do your share of the dishes each meal if you haul all the water."

"Deal!" I jumped at the chance to get out of doing the dishes. I consider myself as having a strong constitution, but there's something about half-chewed, dried-up food that knots my stomach. Katie and I sealed our arrangement by spitting into the palms of our hands and shaking on it.

Now might be the time to 'fess up: I hadn't given much thought to my gramps before. Truth be told, I know my old bloodhound, Jeb, better than I know my mama's daddy. If *I* tend to do things different, Gramps tends to do them downright odd. He was always working on some scheme or another, thinking he'd strike gold. (And I'm talking plain talk here—it's been said the old man once dug up his creek bed in search of gold nuggets.) His crazy dealings with the park were just him chasing more rainbows, Aunt Lydia said. Mama gets so fed up with him and his antics that we've gone for months without checking in on him. That's how I knew Mama was death-scared to move to Knoxville; she'd'a never chosen this old coot over Pop otherwise.

I'd seen Cove folks hugging and kissing on their mamaws and papaws, but my only living grandparent was Gramps. He's not much on giving sugar. He's not much on giving anything but orders. Mama said that wasn't always the case, that when Granny was alive, she'd made him walk the line. Said he even used to be funny. But now—well, now he's just the cranky old-timer in the corner. So he steered clear of us and we steered clear of him. It was a right nice relationship.

But now all that was about to change. Mama buzzed around the place, determined to turn this log pile into a home. She was so contented, humming and puttering about, that I knew she was happy we'd be staying in the Cove. She'd managed to put off Knoxville for as long as Gramps needed us, and from the looks of things, that could be a good while. A good while longer without my pop.

Mama decorated some plain cotton potato sacks by laying some flowers and leaves on them and sprinkling them with ashes. Once she lifted off the live stuff, the pattern left behind was right pretty. She tacked these over the window, and you'd'a thought she'd ordered those curtains right out of Sears and Roebuck.

Next she hammered in a nail or two and hung up some of Pop's best artwork, and it really spiffed up the place. Pop's paintings of Cades Cove look so real, it was like Mama had gone and cut more windows in this place. I smiled. At least we had this part of him here.

Mama also flipped through some of her old *Good Housekeeping* and *National Geographic* magazines and tore out the handsomest photographs. Those were tacked up, too. The effect was a big improvement over the mossy logs underneath.

Gramps stomped in and out of his house the whole time, muttering and sputtering and being overall crotchety. "Curtains?" he'd spew, and trudge out of the house, only to return ten minutes later. "Pitchers?"

Once all our stuff was moved in and Mama was satisfied with her home improvements, she set to making supper. Boy, she must've been out to show Gramps just what he'd signed on for, because she made fried chicken and green beans with ham hocks and mashed potatoes with gravy and juicy sliced tomatoes and corn bread with molasses and even a big cherry pie.

Gramps slunk in toward the end of her preparations and before he could help himself, a twinkle flashed in those grumpy old eyes. He caught himself, though, and hitched up his overalls before plunking into a chair. "Better clean up this mess, Martha."

Mama just smiled and placed a platter of fried okra in front of him. She sat and grabbed Katie's hand on one side and my hand on the other. Katie and I looked across the table at each other. Then Katie shrugged and reached out to take hold of Gramps's hand, but it was already attached to a fork, and it was already shoveling food into his mouth as fast as a waterwheel.

"Daddy!" Mama whispered. "*After* grace."

Gramps made a face like he'd just eaten a slug and dropped his fork into his mashed potatoes. He snatched up my hand, then Katie's. His grasp took me aback, his hand was so strong and smooth.

"Amen," Mama said. We ate like it was the Last Supper, and to me and Katie, it felt like it was. (Heaven help me for making such a comparison, but it's durn near true!) I guess I'd never noticed it, but boy, was Gramps ever something to look at while he was eating—or rather, *not* to look at. He ate way too big, and he made way too much noise, and he left a greasy ring of food bits all round his plate. I thought Katie just might throw up, and even if she had, it still would've been a toss-up between her and Gramps as to who was the most disgusting at the table.

After cleaning his plate, Gramps burped and leaned back in his chair, picking his teeth with a chicken bone. "Girls, there will be no free rides round this homestead, you hear? I got a list of chores a mile long. Autumn, let's start with you."

Have you ever smelled a flock of geese in the summertime? I mean, really *smelled* one? It smells like what I imagine a dead body smells like. Not sure why I think that, exactly, except that wherever there's a flock of geese, there's a cloud of feather dander and puddles of poo that stink like rot. Rotten to the core, they are.

I hate geese. To be fair, I hate all birds. I imagine that they'll peck my eyes out. Got this fear of beaks, you see. I know, I know . . . it's a stupid fear. But anybody who's ever seen a chickenhawk tear apart a skunk with one mighty *riiiiip* might think otherwise about pointing the finger of ridicule at old Autumn Winifred Oliver.

So seeing as how I hate geese and all, I shouldn't have been one bit surprised at my first detail at Camp Gramps.

"Autumn," he told me. "Tomorrow you're on goose duty."

Goose duty? Dang it!

"Keep them out of the garden till your mama and I get back from the barn."

What? Mama had promised I could go fishing tomorrow! "But Mama said—"

"Your mama needs to come to the barn, Autumn. I got big plans for that barn. Don't give me lip."

And so the following day, they left. Left me with a flock of stinking, honking geese. I sat outside on a dusty patch of yard in the sweltering sunlight and thought about how a dip in Abrams Creek would feel right now. Every now and then, I'd have to shoo a goose away from Gramps's withering tomato plants. One little chicken wire fence would solve this problem lickety-split. But I didn't have any chicken wire on hand. Jeez . . . what a crummy job. There must be a better way to stop those nasty geese from chomping down on those scraggly leaves. I got hotter and hotter, and it wasn't because of no sunshine.

And then it hit me. Maybe it was the heat or the dust or the feather dander, but suddenly it occurred to me that the problem here was those durned beaks. If I could somehow rig those orange honkers, they couldn't eat up Gramps's garden. So I scurried around the dusty yard, gathering handfuls of sticks and twigs. And then I set out to catch me some geese.

I do things different. It helps to remind yourself of that when you're wrangling a flock of geese.

I managed to snag every single goose out there, despite a lot of flapping and honking and stinking. And then came the hard part. I pried open those horrible beaks, snipped off a bit of twig, and propped open each goose's mouth like a pup tent. Boy, what a sight! Those stinking geese couldn't close their mouths, let alone do so around a juicy tomato plant. Problem solved.

Those twelve geese looked at each other like they'd all been told they were next on the chopping block, the way their mouths hung open. I couldn't help myself. "Surprise!" I yelled at them, and I laughed to high heaven when they all whipped their heads in my direction, their maws gaping.

Time to fish.

It's a curious thing, guilt. Because there I was, lolly-gagging the afternoon away on the banks of Abrams Creek with cool, clear mountain water lapping at my ankles, and all I could think about was those durn geese. Would their tongues dry up? What if they got lockjaw? Did they need to spit?

"Dang it!" I muttered, and found myself packing up my fishing basket and trudging the mile and a half back home.

It was only four o'clock, so I had plenty of daylight left. Katie wouldn't be home; she was off making jam with Linda McCauley. And I figured I'd beat Gramps and Mama home easy; Gramps'd want to squeeze every drop of sunshine out of the day, cheap as he was. But when the trail came out of the thick trees into the dusty yard, he and Mama were both there. And they were standing beside an *automobile*!

"Wow!" I dropped my fishing basket and pole and ran over to the gleaming black sedan. My hand floated over the boxy back end, down the side of the auto to the dusty runners, around the hump of the spare tire, and finally came to rest on the cowl lights. I huffed on the shiny chrome grille and polished off the cloud of breath with my elbow, just for effect. "Wow!"

In the mirrored bumper I saw a figure appear over my shoulder. "Please, no breathing on the Ford."

I turned and found myself facing a silky smooth

red tie with a gold stickpin dead center. I followed that ribbon of red right up to the man's creamy white face. His hair was as glossy black as his automobile, and his mustache was so thin, it looked as though the whiskers had been left behind by mistake.

Gramps grabbed the gentleman's hand and pumped it in a vigorous handshake. "Mighty nice to finally meet you, Colonel Chapman. The work you've been doing on the national park is right impressive. Right impressive. When I read in the newspaper you were thinking of a park in these parts, I just knew I had to lend my support. That's why I sent you that letter. Glad I could be of help."

The colonel shifted his gaze from Gramps to Mama, apparently cueing her to chime in. Mama hesitated. "This park just sounds so . . ." She fanned herself with her fingertips. "It's such a big change. You're certain that Daddy'll be able to live here in the Cove once the park opens next year?"

A smile grew across Colonel Chapman's face, and I thought he might be one of the handsomest men I'd ever lay my eyes on again. Now I knew why Mama was all fanning herself and whatnot. "Of course. Your father and everyone else in the Cove can stay right where they are. The only thing that will change will be the number of opportunities available to those who live here. Why, Cove residents can open hotels and restaurants and gasoline stations and gift stores. They can stay here and get rich. There's a lot of money to be made in tourism. Indeed, someone has to be here to rake in all the money the tourists are itching to spend."

Gramps hee-hawed and slapped his knee in a too-big gesture. "Itching to spend! Haw! Guess you could say that we here in the Cove got the calamine lotion for that itch."

The colonel's face didn't even twitch, just stayed put in that gleaming smile. "And I assure you that the five million dollars pledged by *John D. Rockefeller* will be put to good use." The colonel laid thick on the name Rockefeller, as if we should pay homage to this fella rather than the five million dollars he'd ponied up. Five *million*. Cash money. My chin nearly hit the ground on that one.

The colonel turned crisply. "Well, my nephew and I must continue our rounds." With that, he swooshed his wrist toward the automobile, and for the first time I noticed a squirrelly-headed boy with thick, thick, thick glasses peering all moony-eyed at me over the door's edge. He looked scrawny and bookish and whiny—all the necessary ingredients a kid needs to get picked on.

"Cody here will be one of your new neighbors," the colonel said in an all-too-cheery kind of voice. I reckon he was aiming that comment at me. "He's never been to the Cove before. He'll stay here with his aunt Matilda over the next few months. I myself will be coming and going while we finalize the deal with FDR."

At the mention of our revered President Roosevelt, Mama sucked in her breath. "You *know* Mr. Roosevelt?" she asked, blushing.

The colonel grinned. "Yes, Mrs. Oliver. If you'd like, I can pass along your good wishes to him and Mrs. Roosevelt."

I thought Mama might pass out at the idea of her name being spoken in the very presence of the First Lady. "Oh, would you?" she breathed, clasping her hands together. "I'd be much obliged."

And then, either in the fervor of the moment or in the excitement of the park or in sheer all-out craziness, my mama said something I'll never, ever forget. Or forgive. She laid her hand on my head and said, "Autumn here would be delighted to show your nephew—Cody, is it?—around the Cove while he gets settled in."

What? I'm not one to have a bunch of pals hanging around, like Katie does. I whipped my head back toward the auto, and that moony-eyed little booger nodded his big head and grinned to beat all. And then the fresh little creep winked at me—winked!

"Excellent. He'll be going to school here, too. I know he'd enjoy a buddy." A *buddy?* Jeez.

The colonel then slid into his car and looked up at Gramps. "Your assistance in bringing this park to life is much appreciated, Mr. Tipton. I was delighted to receive your letter in which you offered your support. I look forward to the town meeting you've organized tomorrow. Once you explain the numerous ways that the park will benefit your neighbors, they will quickly hop on board, I'm sure. I doubt we can win the support of the Cove inhabitants without your endorsement. Cove people tend to be . . . *limited* in scope."

If by that he means that Cove folks on the whole *don't* do things different, well, then I'd have to say I agree.

The colonel cranked his engine. Gramps cupped

his hands around his mouth and shouted above the roar. "Thanks again, Colonel! Folks in this here Cove are about to see big change."

The three of us stood there as that black beauty of an auto stirred up a cloud of dust and vanished. Gramps was smiling until he saw me. His face fell.

Uh-oh . . . the geese! There was no telling what kind of punishment my gramps might dole out for this one.

But instead, Gramps's face pulled into the slightest of grins. "Autumn, fix those durned birds. If we're going to turn this place into a tourist trap, we can't have a bunch of gaping geese flapping around."

3

**I do things different.
It helps to remind
yourself of that
when you sniff out
the skunk, and the
skunk is your kin.**

Last week, before his little brush with death, Gramps
had posted signs all over the Cove:

Come Discuss Our National Park!!!
See What's in Store for You:
Easy Work!!!
Easy Money!!!
Easy Living!!!
Meet at the Schoolhouse
Saturday Next at Noon to
Stake Your Claim to the Riches!!!

But even with that enticing message, only a handful of homeowners showed up, maybe because of the early August thunderstorm howling outside. I certainly wouldn't have been there if Mama hadn't made me come. Katie had her sewing circle, and I'm apparently too "unpredictable" to leave by myself all day.

A stupid town meeting! Who cares about this crummy park, anyways? I stomped all the way to the front of the one-room schoolhouse and slumped onto the bench next to Mama. Neighbors ambled into the tiny white frame building, shook off like wet dogs, and chatted each other up before Gramps ushered them to their seats. Colonel Chapman planted himself on the back right corner bench, arms folded across his broad chest. He somehow managed to be the only dry person in the room. Even Cody, seated next to him, was rain-soaked. Cody looked skimpier than a piece of hay floating in a bucket of water. I slouched lower in the bench. I didn't think he'd seen me, but then he waved at me so hard I thought his fingers might fly off. He stood and walked over. Dang it!

"Hi."

His voice was deeper than I'd expected, kinda

32

froggy. He plunked into the bench too close to me. He was all sticky and steamy, like hot summer rain.

Mama was chewing the fat with big fat Aunt Lydia, to her left. This was my chance to set things straight. I propped my feet up on the bench in front of me and whispered out of the corner of my mouth, "Look, I know my mama told you I'd show you around, but I'm not much for sidekicks. Got it?"

Mama knocked my feet off the bench. Cody's face pulled to one side, and I couldn't tell if he was grimacing or grinning.

Gramps rapped on the blackboard with his knuckles. "Welcome, folks, welcome! So, let's get started." He leaned over, placing his hands atop his knees, and stood in a stoop, like we were a bunch of little kids he was talking to. "What would you say to working half the time for twice the money?" His voice dropped to a husky whisper, as if he was letting us in on some big secret.

No one answered. This meeting was duller than watching paint dry. I pulled an apple from my pocket and bit into it with a huge crunch. "I'd say folks'd be crazy to say no to that," I said, and a chunk of apple flew out of my mouth. Mama dug her elbow into my ribs.

Gramps flung his wrist at Tilly McBroom. "Tilly? You got a good sixty years under your belt."

"Fifty!" Tilly shot back.

I snorted, and when I did, apple shot up my nose.

Gramps ignored me huffing and hacking and Mama pounding me on the back. "Fifty," he said, rolling his eyes. "You want to keep plowing those same fields the rest of your years? Selling honey and molasses off your back porch to tourists sure would be easier than plowing the back forty, right, Tilly?"

Tilly shrugged.

"And Beef," Gramps said, spinning to the hulk of a man in the front row. "You can fix anything with moving parts, right?"

I stopped hacking long enough to sputter, "Ol' Beef's the best!"

"Autumn . . . ," Mama said under her breath.

Beef grinned and winked at me. "You got that right."

"Wouldn't you like to get your hands on one of them fancy automobile engines?" Gramps asked him.

Beef nodded hungrily.

"With this national park, you can do those things," Gramps said. He crossed his arms over his chest and a smug look overtook his face, like he'd made his point and that was that.

"Uh, Tom?" Uncle John Too eased his hand in the air. "How exactly is a national park gonna let us do those things?" A few others in the crowd nodded.

Gramps huffed, like he was going to have to explain this all over again. "When the Great Smoky Mountains National Park opens next year, the park boundaries will stretch down to the northeast corner of the Cove." Gramps raised his eyebrows at Colonel Chapman in the back of the room. I turned to look at him: every last hair was combed neatly into place, and his suit was as crisp as paper. What a dude! The colonel nodded. Cody shifted beside me.

"So us in the Cove is in a lucky spot," Gramps said. He grabbed a hunk of chalk and drew a rough map on the blackboard: two circles, barely overlapping. I gathered that the large circle on top was the park and the small circle at the bottom was the Cove.

"The people visiting the park—all them tourists—are going to need places to sleep, eat, and get gasoline for their autos." He drew arrows going up through the Cove and into the park. I guessed those arrows were supposed to be the droves of visitors entering the park. He dropped the chalk on the teacher's desk. "The money is coming right to our doorsteps. Ain't that so, Colonel?"

Everyone turned to look at Colonel Chapman, who nodded coolly. Cody shifted again. I got the impression his uncle made him downright itchy.

"We all stay in our houses, even keep farming if we want," Gramps said. "So see, nothing will change, unless you want to rake in a ton of extra cash money."

"That's it?" big fat Aunt Lydia whined, and her jowls jiggled. "That's why we slogged through this downpour? To learn nothing will change?"

Jeez. How's that any different? Nothing's changed in the Cove for a million years. I looked at Gramps's map a little closer. "Hey!" I shouted, and leapt up. "That's a right nice depiction of a black widow devouring her young!"

The crowd bust out laughing. *Now* the meeting was hopping! Mama took me by the elbow and led me toward the back door. But as she did, something caught my ear: the sound of teeth sucking.

I'd come to discover that Gramps always sucks his teeth before he stretches the truth. Pop calls this a "tell," 'cause it tells you when someone is bluffing.

I looked back over my shoulder as Mama pulled me to the door.

Gramps was up front nodding and sucking his teeth to beat all. He was getting all worked up over this park, and I had no idea why. "Yep. Guess you're right, Lydia. Nothing will change. So if none of you objects, come on up here and sign this little document that says you're all in favor of a national park in east Tennessee." He tapped an ink pen on a piece of paper lying on the desk.

No one else seemed to know that teeth sucking was Gramps's tell, 'cause a line formed around that paper lickety-split. "Wait a second!" I yelled, but Mama was shoving me out the door onto the soggy front stoop.

"Get outside now, Autumn. You've said your piece."

As the door eased shut, I watched Colonel Chapman and Gramps shake hands while my neighbors signed in favor of a national park. *That old geezer is up to something, and I'm going to find out what.*

"You wanna share my umbrella?"

Right after I ditch Cody.

The following day was a Sunday, and Mama decided that Gramps needed some churching.

"I ain't been to church in years. I reckon the Lord done took me off the roll sheet," Gramps grumbled.

"The Lord don't take nobody off the roll sheet," Mama said, and swatted his arm with her Bible. "Get dressed."

So we put on our Sunday bests, grabbed our birth Bibles, and lined up at the door. There Gramps stood, still in his overalls, empty-handed.

"Daddy, where's your Bible?"

Gramps shrugged, and I thought Mama might pop. "You don't know where your Bible is? My word, Daddy!" She marched back into our makeshift bedroom, retrieved her marriage Bible for him, and thrust the well-worn book at him.

We loaded into the wagon, and Gramps steered us toward the Missionary Baptist Church. "And we're all gonna sit together today, like a family," Mama said as the wagon crunched onto the gravel lot below the church.

"What? But I been sitting with Shirley and Linda and Mable since—"

"No lip, Katie. Today we sit together."

And so we filed into our pew: first Mama, then Gramps, then Katie, then me. I didn't mind so much, 'cause I always sit with Mama in church, but Katie drooped like a mushroom. I tried to cheer her up by scratching funny faces into the dry skin on my knee, but she just slumped down further.

Just before the Right Reverend Feezell got to preaching, Cody stumbled across the threshold of the church with his aunt Matilda and plunked down right next to me. He shot me a goofy smile and pushed his glasses up his face. This kid just didn't get it.

"Mama!" Katie whispered. "Why does Autumn get to sit with her friends?"

"He's not my friend!" I whispered around her to Mama, just to make my position here clear.

"Shhh!" Mama said. Katie and me both threw ourselves back against the pew.

The reverend nodded toward Gramps. "Good to see some old friends today." Gramps smirked. Then the reverend held out an uplifted palm toward Mama. "And the Lord takes care of the shepherds who bring home the lost sheep." I thought Mama just might float off the pew. The reverend started his sermon and got all fevery and worked up over a burning bush. As he wound down, he dabbed his sweaty forehead and finished up as he always does: "Anyone have any prayer requests?"

The usual prayers were offered up: good crops, fat hogs, honest living that'll please the Lord. But then Tommy Bledsoe snuck his hand in the air. Tommy Bledsoe, my sworn archenemy ever since a much-begrudged game of Stink Base.

"I got a prayer of mourning."

The crowd murmured. *What's this? A prayer of mourning we knew nothing about?* But the group of kids that sat around Tommy tittered.

"Well, certainly, son. Go ahead," said the reverend.

"Yessir. I'd like to lift one up for the newly departed . . . Autumn Winifred Oliver."

Half the church busted out laughing; the other half clenched their jaws at all this cutting up in church. I myself burned all awkward until out of the corner of my eye, I saw Gramps's shoulders shaking. Then I burned all angry. Here was my gramps— a fella who never went to church, a fella hiding something big about this park—laughing at *me*! In church!

My hand shot into the air, and I leapt up before I could stop myself.

"I'd like to offer up a prayer of thanks," I shouted above the laughter. "I'd like to thank my gramps for all the hard work he's done on the national park." The laughter slowly died down. "He's got nothing but *our best interest* at heart. Right, Gramps?" Every face in the church turned to focus on Gramps.

Not even Gramps could lie in church. Surely I'd just guilted him into 'fessing up this secret of his. But instead, he just grinned and nodded and soaked up all those prayers of thanks like the reverend's burning bush might soak up buckets of water.

"Amen," our neighbors said, shaking their heads in thanks. "Amen."

As we were filing out, Gramps pumped the reverend's hand in a huge handshake. "Now *that* was the best time I ever had in a church pew."

4

I do things different. It helps to remind yourself of that when the cove ghosts start raising a ruckus.

Thunk!

It was sometime after sundown the next day, maybe nine-thirty or so, when we first heard it.

Thump!

Katie was finishing up my share of the dishes, like we'd agreed on. I was sketching Jeb, squeezing my likeness of the mutt into the blank margins of the *Knoxville Sentinel*. I looked up from the snoozing dog and over to Katie. Katie looked over to Mama. Mama looked over to Gramps.

"What was that?" Mama asked, lowering her knitting and raising her eyes to the roof.

"Sounds like—" Katie began.

Thud!

"A *rock*!" I yelled with a laugh. I ran to the one big front window, cupped my hands around my eyes, and pressed them against the pane to see into the darkness outside. Katie appeared right beside me, smudging the wavy glass, too. Who would want to rock us? What had we done now?

Thomp!

Boy oh boy. I bet this had to do with the park. I hadn't yet figured out what Gramps was hiding, but somebody had. Somebody else knew Gramps was up to no good. Somebody was here to make him 'fess up.

"Oh, Lord!" Mama jumped to her feet and joined us at the window. "I knew it. I knew it would come to this."

Thop!

"Lord-a-mercy," Mama cried, grabbing me and Katie by the elbows. "We're being rocked. *Rocked!* I knew we hadn't heard the end of you cussing like a sailor in front of all them ladies, Daddy!" She turned and pointed a finger over her shoulder at Gramps, who snarled from his rocking chair. "They've come to tell us to mend our sinnin' ways!"

Thwack!

Mama cupped her hands around her mouth and yelled out the window. "Forgive us! Forgive us, for we oughta know better than to use the *h*-word—"

" 'Hell,' Martha," Gramps muttered from his rocking chair. "I said 'hell.' " Katie sputtered a giggle, and Mama pinched the back of her arm.

Thud!

"We oughta know better than to use the *h*-word in public, outside the doors of the Lord's house. Our *kind, forgiving neighbors*"—this part she hollered as loud as she could—"should know that we repent. *Repent!*" She got to swaying and shouting so loudly that Jeb joined in, baying along like the fool dog he is. And when Jeb starts to baying, the old mutt passes the worst gas you ever did smell. Katie and me held our noses and fanned our faces as best we could. The folks outside were getting quite a show.

"I'll be dadburned." Gramps jumped from his chair and grabbed his Remington Parker off the wall. He flung open the door and sprang to the edge of the front porch.

"You stay right where you are, you cowards!" he yelled, waving the shotgun over his head like a madman. He leapt off the porch into darkness.

After some rustling and wrestling outside and some fevery baying inside, we soon knew Gramps must've captured at least one of them, because we heard an awful "Ow! Ow! Ow!" grow louder and louder as it got closer and closer to the house.

"Forgive my daddy!" Mama yelled toward the outside.

In the doorway, the shadowy outline of my gramps appeared, silhouetted in that area where dark meets light. He looked downright magical, like how I always pictured one of them singing cowboys on the radio.

"He who casts the first stone," he said with a snort, and pulled a moony-eyed little booger inside by the ear.

Cody!

Mama hurried to the doorway and knelt before the kid, wrapping her hands around his pasty face. "Mercy heavens! Why was you rockin' us, child? What did we do to offend the likes of you?"

Cody looked at Mama like she was speaking Spanish. Or juggling rocks on her tongue. Takes about the same amount of skill to do both, if you ask me.

"You think I got something to hide?" Gramps

growled at him. "What is it you think I need to confess, son?"

Cody swallowed. "Uh, nothing, sir. Just wanted Autumn to come outside, is all." He blushed and kicked the floor with his heel. "Thought I'd get her attention like Romeo did for Juliet." Dang it!

Katie was rubbing that earlobe of hers so fast I thought it might catch fire. "Ooooo, Cody! Autumn here just *loves* a romantic." She shoved me toward the little creep. Double dang it!

"Fool kids oughta know better than to wander round after sunset, rockin' their neighbors," Gramps grumbled while remounting his shotgun. "Like to get hisself shot."

"Yessir," Cody said to the floor.

"You weren't seeking our repentance, son?" Mama asked. Cody shook his head so hard, he looked like he might throw himself off balance. Mama knelt next to him and gently straightened his shirt at the shoulders. " 'Cause throwing rocks at a house? It means you think the folks inside got something to regret."

I thought Cody might pass out with embarrassment.

Mama cocked her head. "You not carryin' a

lantern?" she asked. Cody shook his head again. "Why, how on earth did you find your way?"

"Wasn't easy, ma'am." He swallowed and his voice returned. "But the moon's big tonight. Back in Knoxville, streetlights come on at dusk. Guess I didn't think about how dark it'd be here after sunset."

I thought Mama might cry at the thought of this crazy kid wandering around the Cove at night. "My heavens, boy! That's a mite dangerous. Does your auntie know you're here?"

Again, Cody shook his head at the floor. Gramps groaned.

"Well, looks like Daddy's gonna have to hitch up the wagon and take you back home," Mama said, eyeballing Gramps with one of her do-it-or-else looks.

"Oh, no, ma'am, please!" Cody breathed, and I couldn't tell if it was because he didn't want to be a nuisance or because he didn't want to be alone with Gramps. "Can't you just send word?"

We all got a quick chuckle out of that one. "Boy, by the time we send word you're here, we could already have you home." She shook her head at the mere notion. "Send word!"

Then she turned to me. "Autumn, you're going, too."

Katie spit a giggle. "A moonlight ride with your boyfriend! How *romantic*!" She made smoochy kissy noises.

"Hush, you!" I hissed, but I was secretly kinda excited. After all, it wasn't every day I got to go on a midnight ride.

So before I knew it, Cody and I were cocooned under two of Mama's softest quilts, lying on our backs in the rear of the cart. We passed 'neath stars that looked like hundreds of silver coins flung across a black velvet night sky. Gramps steered the team of horses across the Cove, cutting through the wheat fields, and the *swish-swish-swish* of the stalks and the sweet yellow smell of the buds and the swaying of the cart made it difficult to stay awake. Luckily (ha!) I had Cody for that.

"I think this park will be the prettiest park that ever was. My uncle says nothing in the world compares to east Tennessee, and I believe him on that. He says he's going to make everyone in the Cove really rich since he's helping bring in the national park and y'all will be right on the park's border and will be able to open hotels and restaurants and auto-mobile gasoline stations for all the tourists." Seeing no reaction from me, he asked, "Aren't you excited about being rich?"

I shrugged. If he only knew that I'd pay just about any sum to get to Knoxville and start *really* living.

"So why's your name Autumn?" he asked. "Your hair's blond, not red."

"I fall a lot." At this, Gramps snorted from his driver's perch.

"You born in the fall?"

"No."

"Where's your dad?"

"Where's *your* dad?"

At that, he fell silent. Served him right, the nosy little booger. But after a while, I could tell he was sad. Real sad. I couldn't tell if he was crying (I didn't really look), but it wasn't cold enough out there for those kind of sniffles.

I sighed, propped myself up on one elbow, and looked at him. "My pop works for the Little River Lumber Company, and so he's gone a lot, and it really stinks 'cause he's the best baseball player and banjo player and artist I know."

Cody nodded, and so I laid back down and started thinking about how if I could capture all those silver-coin stars, I'd be rich, all right.

"Hey—that uncle of yours?" I asked, picturing the colonel's gleaming white smile in the stars.

"Yeah?"

"He sure don't seem like he hails from Cades Cove."

"He doesn't. Comes from Knoxville. He's my great-uncle, dad's side."

"No relation to your aunt Matilda?"

"Second cousin, mom's side."

I nodded into the darkness. Knoxville. So *that's* why the colonel's so sophisticated. I knew there was no way that fella was related to the Matilda Ogle I'd known my whole life.

"Sounds like you know a lot of your relatives," I said, though I wasn't sure why I cared to make such small talk.

"No. Not really."

"You're from Knoxville, too, though."

"No. I just lived there a few years."

"I bet it's about the greatest place on earth."

Cody shrugged. "It's not bad for the Underwear Capital of the World."

Gramps huffed a laugh.

"What?"

"Knoxville. It's called the Underwear Capital of the World."

"No, it's not!"

"Yeah, it is. Lots of textile mills there."

"You don't know!"

"Yeah, I do. I worked in one of them for two years."

This kid's worked in a textile mill? Pop says that's about the hardest job there is. Says the cloth fibers stick to you for days, like spiderwebs. "Well, I can't wait to move there," I said in a huff, "Underwear Capital or not."

We laid there a minute more in silence.

"Ever see fireworks?" Cody asked.

"Nope. You?"

"Yeah." He paused for a minute. "Nothing compared to all these stars, though."

Huh. I was just about to drift off to sleep when it occurred to me that this kid was crazier than a toad with a tail.

And then what sounded like a lady's scream ripped through the cool night air.

"Well, I'll be," Gramps said with a laugh. "If it

ain't ole Mavis Estep, coming back from the dead for her cussing quilt."

Cody like to have jumped out of his skin. "Back from the dead?"

But me, I was more excited about that second part. (I mean, according to those church bells and every last one of my neighbors, I'd already come back from the dead. Big deal.)

"Cussing quilt?" I asked. Maybe we were about to hear Gramps tear through some more juicy words! And in front of the colonel's nephew, too. Boy, would Mama be stomping mad about this one!

"Yep," Gramps said, and sucked his teeth. *Uh-oh. Here we go.*

"Yep. Old Mavis Estep sure did love her quilts. 'Specially that cussing quilt. See, Mavis was born in a thunderstorm. Like to have wiped out the Cove, that storm. Anyway, a baby born in a storm such as that is fated to be struck by lightning. Everybody knows that."

Cody looked at me with wide eyes, and so I nodded. What the hey. I can play along.

"The old girl was so scared of a stray lightning bolt, she wouldn't even hold a spoon if there was a single gray cloud in the sky. So they's no way Mavis would sleep in a metal bed. Might get fried in her sleep, you see."

Cody shivered and huddled under his blanket. I was getting flustered. "What about that cussing quilt?"

Gramps smiled over his shoulder at us from his perch on the driver's bench. His tobacco-stained teeth glinted in the moonlight. "I'm getting there, missy, hold on. Mavis's husband, Basil, used to make such fun of the old girl and her jitters! So Mavis did what all the ladies do—she made a quilt, and with each stitch, she cussed that teasing husband of hers. See, she loved Basil, and 'stead of getting mad at him, she'd take it out on the quilt. Worked on that quilt an awful lot, she did. That cussing quilt like to have saved that marriage, I'd say. So it was surely among her favorites."

Just then, another wail rolled over the wheat field. I had to admit it was getting pretty creepy out there. I don't believe in ghosts or haints or none of that hooey, but I sure didn't know where that lonely scream was coming from.

"So what happened to the quilt?" Cody asked.

Gramps flipped his switch at the lead horse to steer the animals to the left toward a faint, flickering light. "Old Mavis died an early death, and not 'cause of no lightning. No, the croup got that one. On her deathbed, Mavis told Basil that her only wish was that he should never, ever place her prized cussing quilt on a metal bed. Ever."

"So of course he did it, right?" I asked.

Gramps chuckled. "Of course. Basil's second wife, Trulie, sure did love that cussing quilt. It only took a few cold Cove nights before all of Trulie's nagging and complaining convinced him to put that big, warm quilt on their new bed. The first night that quilt was on a metal bed, Trulie awoke to the ghost of Mavis standing at the foot of the bed, screaming her scream, like we just heard. Cussing a blue streak, she was."

"Really?" I asked, and pulled my knees under me. A *lady* cussing a blue streak? *Now* we were getting somewhere!

"Sure," Gramps said. "Happened for two straight nights. Course, Basil thought Trulie was being a foolish old biddy, claiming to see haints and all that. So that stubborn old coot kept that quilt on that bed just to spite her. On the third night, Mavis had had enough. It was a night a lot like tonight, not a cloud in the sky," he said, swishing his hand above his head. "Sound asleep they were, Basil and Trulie, when out of nowhere, a bolt of lightnin' streaked down from the clear sky and fried old Basil right there in his pajamas. Zap!" he shouted, zigzagging his finger toward the sky. Cody started.

"Trulie hightailed it outta there," he continued. "When she returned with her papa, Basil's bones were melted to that old metal bed, but the prized cussing quilt that had been over their cold bodies was folded neatly in the corner, not a singe on it."

I shuddered. Tall tale or not, that was one spooky story.

"Yep. Folks say old Mavis still haints these here parts, screaming and cussing and looking for that prized quilt."

Cody cleared his throat. "What did it look like? The quilt, I mean?"

"Oh, it was a real beauty. Red squares on a white backdrop . . . kinda like the one you're huddled under *right now*!" Gramps jerked around and pointed at us as he said that. I jumped, and Cody leapt out of that quilt quicker than a jackrabbit on hot gravel.

Gramps laughed so hard his eyes disappeared into slits and his hand slapped his right knee. I laughed, too, and finally Cody began to laugh with us. We were struggling to catch our breath when we heard the scream again. Cody looked at me, real scared-like, and I shrugged. I'd never heard such a fierce wail before, either. Maybe it really was old Mavis?

"Just in the nick of time," Gramps said, and steered the cart onto the dusty trail that led to Cody's aunt's house. "Wouldn't want *us* to get struck by no lightning." Before we knew it, Cody jumped out of the moving cart and ran into the arms of his aunt Matilda, who had flung open the front door.

"Oh, Auntie!" he said in a breath, and searched the sky for possible stray lightning bolts. "I'm so sorry. I would've never wandered away if I'd known about old Mavis Estep!"

Miss Matilda raised a single eyebrow at Gramps, who was still perched on the driver's bench of the cart. He shrugged.

"Mavis Estep, eh?" she said. "I suppose you know that's just an old tall tale."

"But we *heard* her!" Cody whined. "Didn't we, Autumn?" I nodded.

"What you *heard* was a panther," Miss Matilda said, pulling her nephew closer to her. "I heard him, too. Was I ever worried!"

"A panther?" I asked. I'd never heard one in all my eleven years of living here, though I'd heard they used to raise quite a ruckus. I looked at Gramps. He rolled his eyes and looked the other way.

"Not many of them critters around much anymore," Miss Matilda said. "In my day, you couldn't sleep some nights for all the screaming." She laughed, and her tight face loosened into a sly grin. "Tom, you ain't changed one bit since our school days. Why don't you and your girl come inside and tell us some more lies?"

"Can't," Gramps said, and picked up the horse whip. And then he sucked his teeth long and hard. *Uh-oh.*

"Gotta get home to Martha. She fell and broke her arm yesterday."

I narrowed my eyes at Gramps. The skunk—he can't help himself! Cody looked confused, but he didn't say nothing. I suppose the fact that Gramps had pointed a rifle at him earlier that evening kept his mouth sealed shut.

"What?" Miss Matilda said, placing a hand on her chest. "Oh, my! Is there anything I can do to help?"

"Well . . ." Gramps slid his eyes toward me real

slow-like. "I suppose she's having some trouble round the kitchen."

Miss Matilda thrust her chin in the air. "Well, I'll just round up the girls and we'll tote over some meals for y'all. Tell her not to worry about a thing. We've got your next twenty or so meals covered. A broken arm—oh, my!"

Gramps smiled and switched the lead horse. "Mighty nice of you, Matilda." And when we rode away, Gramps was whistling and smiling and sucking his teeth.

5

I do things different.
It helps to remind
yourself of that
when you hear
the sinners and the
saints whistling
the same ditty.

Fried chicken and sweet milk and stewed corn and apple jelly and white beans and cracklin' bread and stewed parsnips and horehound candy and green grape pie and hominy and fried cucumbers and leather britches beans and corn dodgers and hole-up cabbage and blackberry cobbler. Mama accepted it all with a sheepish grin over Gramps's little prank. But when our guests left, she packaged it up for Katie to tote over to Tilly McBroom, "who needs it way more than we do."

"Dagnabbit, Martha!" Gramps sputtered, and

paced his tiny cabin after Mama packed up a supper of ham hocks and corn bread and fried potatoes. "That food is for you!"

Mama raised her eyebrows at him like only my mama can, and her brown eyes flared. "You lied. That there is a sinner's supper."

Gramps's mouth bunched up into a tiny knot on one side of his face, and the toothpick he sucked stuck out like an exclamation point. "How many times do I have to tell you, Martha? She *asked* for a lie. Didn't she, girl?" He jerked his head in my direction.

Much as I hated to, I had to nod. It was true, after all. Cody, who had started hanging round our home like that one pesky housefly you just can't swat, nodded, too. I scowled at him.

"So the way I sees it," Gramps said, toothpick bouncing around his wrinkled lips, "we deserve that food. Forced me into a lie, that cunning devil Matilda Ogle." Cody giggled.

Mama folded her arms across her chest. I knew from experience that meant the end of this discussion. Gramps heaved a big, showy sigh and stormed out of the cabin.

Cody jerked his head in the direction of the door. I shrugged. Why not? I still hadn't figured out what

Gramps was hiding about the park, so a little snooping around might uncover something. We snuck out behind Gramps and followed him into the thick woods.

After we walked about a quarter of a mile through cool darkness, the leafy canopy yawned open and we stood at the edge of a grassy clearing. The sudden sunlight burned my eyes. When my sight cleared, I made out four white boxes, each one on stilts, each one about the size of Mama's washing tub, each one buzzing.

Bees! Gramps lifted the lid off one of the beehives and plunged his arm in up to his elbow.

Cody gasped. "Mr. Tipton, be . . ."

Careful. I finished Cody's thought in my head. Dang it! So much for being a sneak.

Plump bees climbed up Gramps's arm, clung to his chest, crawled on his face, swarmed in his hair. Bees dotted his body like a fuzzy black rash.

"Don't worry, son," he whispered. He apparently knew we'd been trailing him the whole time. "Me and these bees, we got an understanding. They don't sting me and I don't squash them."

Well, I'll be a monkey's uncle, I thought. *Old Gramps is a bee charmer!*

Gramps grinned at us and pulled a dripping, golden honeycomb out of the box. "Autumn, bring me one of them jars," he whispered, pointing his chin at a pile of Ball jars stowed under one of the bee houses. I shook my head. No way was I getting near those things.

Gramps scowled at me. I felt bumps come up on my skin like the chicken I was. But if that wasn't enough, I'll be dadburned if that little booger Cody didn't step up and fetch one of those jars. The show-off!

Gramps took the jar from Cody and slid the oozing honeycomb inside. The jar soon filled with honey seeping from the waxy comb. The bees flew off Gramps and back to their bee homes.

Gramps sat under a nearby oak and patted the ground next to him. He drew out a jackknife from the pocket of his overalls, cut off a piece of the honey-comb, and handed it to Cody. "A treat for your brav-ery." I couldn't believe my ears. *I* was the brave one here. Wasn't I?

Cody smiled and took the honeycomb and looked at it stupidly. "You chew it, dummy," I said.

Gramps cut off a piece of honeycomb for me. "A treat 'cause you let a city boy get the best of you." Ooooo! My insides cramped up. But I deserved the rib-bing, I suppose. Me, outdone by a city kid. Dang it!

We sat there a long time, chewing the sweet honey-comb and listening to the soft hum of the tiny bugs. I counted how many times I could crack my knuckles, while Cody pushed his toe through the dirt, unearthing rocks and pocketing the good ones. He finally broke the silence.

"You don't really have an understanding with those bees, do you, Mr. Tipton?"

Gramps moved the big lump of wax he was working on to one cheek. "Nah. That's a story, boy."

We sat there a long time again before Cody asked, "What's your favorite story, Mr. Tipton?"

It was a good question. Maybe, I thought, he'd pick a story about the moonshiners in Chestnut Flats. I hear they have houses right on the Tennessee–North Carolina border, and when the police come knocking, the criminals just walk into a different room—because they're in a different state, they can't be touched. Or maybe he'd choose the story of him and his brother getting caught in a snowstorm and surviving three days in a hollowed-out tree (Mama'd told us that one). Or maybe he even had some good outhouse-tipping tales. Who knows? A geezer as old as Gramps probably had dozens of shady friends and ripe yarns.

Gramps scratched his chin. "Well, now, let's see. Guess I'd have to say my favorite story is 'bout Adam and Eve and the Garden of Eden."

"What? You can't pick that!" Maybe I was still smarting from the ribbing, but I didn't think it was fair for somebody who never even went to church to pick a Bible story as his favorite.

"But that story is so sad," Cody said. "Adam and Eve lost everything 'cause of a slimy old snake."

Gramps snapped his fingers at Cody. "There's where you're wrong, boy. Adam and Eve lost everything 'cause that was their choice. 'Member how that story ends?"

"Well, sure," I said. "They get greedy and it gets them kicked out of paradise."

"No, I mean before that."

"They eat the apple."

Gramps heaved a big sigh. "*After* that."

I shrugged, but Cody nodded. "They gain the knowledge of good and evil. They see what's right and what's wrong."

Gramps picked his teeth with his penknife. "Way I see it, that was likely the intent all along."

I kicked at a clod of dirt. This was just like Sunday school. Worse—at least in Sunday school I didn't get one-upped by a city kid. No, make that *two*-upped. I really could've used a good outhouse-tipping tale just about then.

Later that day, I decided to hike up to Abrams Falls. Normally, I'd tote up my fishing pole and basket, but today I opted for the company of my sketch pad and pencils. I did *not* opt for the company of Cody, but he was there, too, stumbling up the steep trail behind me.

I draw whenever I'm blue. I'm blue whenever I get to stewing over how crummy it is to be eleven years old. It's a crack in life. Nobody treats me like a grown-up, but they hate it when I act like a kid. When we'd got home from the beehives, I thought the smart thing to do would be to tell Mama that Gramps is up to something suspicious with this park. She'd hushed me up quicker than she'd shush a church talker and told me to respect my elders. Jeez!

I sat Indian-style on a slick black rock next to the falls. When the wind changed direction, the spray blew on me and the cold water pricked my skin like tiny needles. It felt good, though, the cool beads biting the edge off the hot August day. My sketch pad caught a few drops now and then, warping the paper in tiny dots. I got a little sadder then, watching the paper buckle. Drawing always reminds me of Pop. He's the best artist in these parts. Everybody says so.

The falls were shadowy that day, with more deepy darks than the last time I'd sketched them. Cody scampered around like a diseased squirrel, collecting those dumb rocks of his. His pockets bulged with the weight of so many rocks, he had to keep hitching up his pants. All his rustling distracted me from my sketch. For some reason, I grew itchy-irritated watching him sock those darn rocks away. What a stupid hobby!

"Why do you do that?" I asked.

"Huh?"

"Why do you collect rocks?"

Cody shrugged. "I guess because they're pretty much always the same. For the most part, they just stay put."

"Huh. That sounds like everything I know."

"That sounds like heaven to me."

Now that's just plain loopy, liking things because they stay put. So I said so.

Cody pushed his glasses back up his face. He paused so long I half expected him to empty his pockets in defeat. But then he said, "My mom's really sick. I've stayed with lots of relatives I don't know while my dad works three jobs to pay her doctor bills. But once she gets better, I'll get to stay put, too. Once she gets better." He stooped and fingered a sharp gray stone.

I didn't know what to say, so I did like I always do

when I don't know what to say: I say something stupid. "I like drawing." Now, how dumb. I was sitting there with my sketch pad. "I like it 'cause it lets me see the same thing in a different way each time."

Boy, was that ever a stupid thing to say. I expected Cody to laugh right at me. But he nodded and flipped over a chipped red rock with his toe. "You like things that are different."

And that's how, against my better judgment, I wound up with a sidekick.

Several days later was the third Thursday of the month. Mama, Katie, and me stood out at the Cove Loop Road with our wheelbarrow. We were waiting to see the cloud of dust on the horizon that signaled the arrival of Jeremiah Butler's rolling store. Of course, Cody was there, too, and he did what fellas always do when Katie is around: jabber without end.

"So I'd guess those movie palace screens are so big, it'd cover Gramps's cabin wholly if you were to lay one atop it." He was talking to me, but he cut his eyes at Katie to make certain she was listening in.

"Really?" Katie breathed.

"Now, Cody, isn't that a bit of an exaggeration?" Mama asked. Mama hates exaggerating more than anyone in the whole world ever has or ever will.

"No, ma'am. Those screens are gargantuan."

I wasn't sure how big *gargantuan* was, but I didn't let on. It sure did sound awfully big.

"So Cody, how much does a movie picture cost?" Katie asked. I could just see her calculating in her head how much it'd cost those Knoxville boys to take her on a date. Katie wants to go on a date so bad she might as well wear a placard stating just that.

"Well, I'm not sure about that, exactly. Me and my cousins, we used to sneak in the back way."

Now how about that! Little old Cody, a bona fide sneak. I gotta admit, I got a soft spot in my heart for sneaks.

"There he is!" Mama said. She lifted her chin at the growing dust cloud and knotted her skirt in her hands. "Right there!"

Mama was excited to see Jeremiah for one reason only: he toted the mail from Knoxville.

Katie noticed Mama's excitement, too. "You getting all worked up about that cornmeal, Mama?" she teased.

"Oh, hush, you." Mama blushed and gave Katie a playful shove.

Jeremiah's truck skidded to a halt before us. He

hopped out of his truck, and the chickens in the coop atop the cab squawked and flapped at the slamming door.

"Mornin', ladies," Jeremiah said, and swooped off his cap for a deep bow. He glanced up at Katie while still bent in half and jerked his head at Cody. "Who's your suitor?"

Katie rolled her eyes at me but clucked over Jeremiah like a mother hen. "Why, this here's nobody—just Cody." At which I thought Cody might shrivel up like a piece of frying fatback. "*Mama* here sure is excited to see you, Jeremiah."

Mama looked to die of embarrassment. "Hush, Kathryn," she said, and I knew she meant it. "Let Jeremiah go about his business."

Jeremiah leapt about like a frog on gigging day. He opened the back hatch, and as usual, his truck was stuffed full—Jeremiah's rolling store carried everything from magazines to lard. He even carried toilet paper! Toilet paper, as if anyone in the Cove was *that* prissy. Even Katie uses normal old newsprint.

After he'd loaded our wheelbarrow with flour and cornstarch and salt, he reached into his large canvas knapsack and pulled out what we'd all been waiting on: the letter from Pop.

Mama ran her fingers over the handwriting on the

front before gently untying the string on the parcel. She handled the letter like it was a baby. As usual, inside the big envelope were three smaller ones: one for Mama, one for Katie, and one for me.

Hiya, Autumn! How's my favorite season? I'm counting down the days till you and Mama and Katie join me in Knoxville. At least, I would count them if I knew when you'd get here. But Gramps needs you, so you help out your mama, you hear? Kin is kin. And when you get here, I got a surprise for you: roller skates!

Roller skates? Mama always said they were a waste of money, that if the good Lord wanted us to roll, He'd have us sprout wheels. Nobody in the Cove had them, anyways, 'cause there was nowhere to use them. But I kept reading. . . .

All the roads round here are paved, so all the kids have them. Boy, I can't wait to see you zipping around on them skates!

Me neither! Skates! *Boy oh boy! I wonder if Mama knows.*

I miss you and Mama and Katie so much it hurts. But this job is really good money, much more than I can make being a farmer. And the way I figure it, I gotta work for this lumber company now, because these fellas can chop down a forest the size of three farms in half a day. There won't be any trees left in a few years. It's ugly, ugly work.

I didn't know what he meant by that. But it sure didn't sound happy.

Mama tells me you've been helping Gramps get his farm ready for the opening of the park. Attagirl! Gramps may be more bitter than dandelion tea, but he's got one heck of an idea with that park. You keep stepping up, you hear? This idea of his might actually work, and if it does, old harebrained Tom Tipton will get the last laugh on us all. Hotels in Cades Cove! Your granddaddy Oliver would never have believed it—he might as well be rolling around heaven on roller skates of his own!

Bear hugs and butterfly kisses,
Pop

6

I do things different.
It helps to remind
yourself of that
when you realize
you've had a hand in
putting your family
in the poorhouse.

I'm about the world's best eavesdropper. If I weren't, I'd never find anything out. But even with all my snooping around, I still hadn't figured out why Gramps would lie about this old park. It all seemed on the up-and-up: park = tourists = money. So I did what Pop said I should do: I helped get ready for the army of tourists headed our way. I could've cared less if them visitors had a comfortable place to bunk. But Gramps thought it'd make him rich, so my list of chores grew longer and longer.

Truth be told, if it hadn't been for all the summer rain we'd been getting of late, old Gramps likely would've worked my fingers to the nubbins with all his tourist-trap preparations. For two weeks he'd been doling out chores to me and Katie and Mama and even Cody. He had us help him take down all the sweet-smelling tobacco in the barn (and when I say help, I mean *we* did it; he'd really gotten used to taking it easy after his little brush with death). Then he had us scour the place with Mama's old hickory mop and some rock sand. We hauled in a few straw mattresses and burlap curtains and plenty of kerosene lamps. We changed that rat trap into a right nice little guest home for all those rich tourists. Gramps even nailed a sign to a fence post along the Cove Loop Road:

Tipton's Lodge and Tourist Camp.
Good Springs, Good Meals,
Clean Cabins.
Drunks and Base Characters Excluded.

But then it rained. And rained. And rained. All the color washed away and everything in the Cove turned mud brown.

"We're gonna have to line up your animals two by two, Daddy," Mama said as a soaking wet Gramps entered the cabin and shook off like an old dog.

"They's no way I'm getting on an ark with the likes of this crew," Katie grumbled from behind the cover of *Anne of Green Gables*. "Nope, my ark is gonna be me, Shirley Tucker, Linda McCauley, and Mable Feezell." She paused, and a light flickered in her eyes. "And maybe Shirley's brother, Jackson," she sang, and clutched the book to her chest. I stuck out my tongue at her.

"Forget the ark," Gramps said. "We'll jest ride McCauley's outhouse into the storm. Floating down Abrams Creek, it is. Right now it's hung up on a tree limb next to the mill."

I jumped up and grabbed the back of Cody's shirt. "Let's go!" He stayed planted, cross-legged, in front of the fire.

"That outhouse must've been twenty yards from the riverbank," Mama said. "Floating, is it?"

"River's flooded again," said Gramps. He fell into his rocker and huffed more rain off his face with a puff of breath. "Real bad this time. Durned lumber companies, it is."

Mama scowled her hush-up scowl at him and

whipped around to the kitchen before I could get a read on her.

"Pop's lumber company?" I asked, still tugging at Cody, the durn lump.

Gramps didn't give one twit about any hush-up looks. "Yep," he said. "And others. The more trees they chop down, the less there is to stop all the rainwater from runnin' down the mountain. Nothin' but a big, muddy mess, those lumber companies make. But all that tree choppin'll stop once the park takes over." He looked real smug when he said this. Mama banged some pans around in the kitchen.

Katie finally looked up from her silly book. "But don't that mean—"

"Yes, Katie," Mama interrupted her. Worry jumped into Mama's eyes. "Your daddy'll lose his job."

It took a second for that to sink in, like I was watching Mama write out the words on a tablet rather than speak them.

Pop . . . lose his *job*? Jobs were mighty hard to come by these days. Where would we live? We'd already sold our house here in the Cove. Would we still move to Knoxville if Pop didn't have work there? Or would we— Oh, dang it! Would we try to run the tourist trap here in the Cove with Gramps?

The muscles in my neck squeezed up. Now I knew Gramps's dirty little secret: his park would shut down all the lumber companies. Lots of folks round here have kin working in those sawmills. Nobody would've signed his official little paper if they'd known they were signing away all those jobs.

And Mama! She looked worried, to be sure, but not the least bit sad.

Cody scrambled to his feet like the fire had leapt out of the fireplace and licked his toes. "C'mon, Autumn," he said. "Let's go check out that floating commode."

He took my wrist and pulled me out the door before I could get my words working again. Katie's voice trailed off behind me: "But I don't understand! Why do we want this old park again?"

I balled up my fists so tight I thought my fingernails might poke straight through the palms of my hands. Twelve minutes earlier I couldn't've given two flips about this old park. I'd even helped prepare for it! Now it was about to tear me to shreds.

I guess I felt numb about the whole mess, because I followed Cody about half a mile through the warm

76

summer rain before I realized he hadn't let go of my wrist, the little sneak. I wriggled my hand out of his. I wasn't about to cozy up to some lousy park supporter.

"Leggo, traitor," I said. Cody looked like he'd been stuck by a pin.

I stomped ahead of him, splashing through the muddy field toward the river. "You and your flashy uncle are gonna put Pop out of a job. And Gramps! Ooooo!" I clenched up my fists again. "When I think about all the work we did for him in that stupid barn. Each chore put us closer to the poorhouse!"

"But Autumn—"

"Don't you 'but Autumn' me, mister!" I said, sounding an awful lot like Mama. I was so mad, I did the first thing I could think to do. I picked up a rock.

I wanted to chuck it at his head. But nah— beaning him with a rock'd be too easy. I bet he wouldn't even duck. I twiddled the rock around in the palm of my hand. It was smooth and pinkish and full of holes—likely one Cody would want for his collection. So I showed it to him.

"Pretty, ain't it?" I said.

"Yeah," he breathed. "It's a hematite."

"It's *you*!" Then I spit on the rock three times

and hurled it over my left shoulder. Stupid, yes, but I felt better.

Cody's eyes grew wide. "Was that some kind of mountain voodoo or something?"

It took everything I had not to laugh in his face. I squinted at him. "Yep. I just put a hex on you and your heart of stone."

"Hex?"

"Yep."

"Wha—what kind of hex?"

I smiled a big, evil smile as he followed me to the mill. "Just have to wait and see. Now *get lost* already!"

A small crowd had gathered on the riverbank opposite the snared outhouse. The shack was wedged in the crook of a tree, and the river rushed all around it. The muddy water trapped inside the outhouse spewed out the door's crescent moon cutout in a neat little arc.

"Ain't she something!" Beef Jackson bellowed. "Looks like a reg'lar fountain, don't she?"

As we all stood admiring the Cove's latest work of art, a squawking squalor came tumbling around the bend upriver.

"What is that?" Tilly McBroom squinted at the thing drifting our way.

"It's a chicken coop!" Beef yelled, and we all shook our heads as the McCauleys' chickens screeched past us in a mess of feathers and mud and chicken wire.

"Poor old McCauley's really going to have a time of it," Tilly said, clicking her tongue. "Bet half his stuff's done washed to Townsend. That man's gonna need all our hands."

"Wait a second," Cody said. "Isn't Mr. McCauley an undertaker?"

And just like that, a coffin tumbled around the bend and washed up practically at our feet.

Beef Jackson grabbed ahold of my arm and pushed me toward the washed-up coffin. "Open it," he whispered.

"Why me?" I squeaked.

"You're the one who's supposed to be layin' in one of them, anyways."

"Uh-*uh*." I shook my head. I bit my lip and took a step back. The crowd looked at the bare pine box as though everyone half expected a dead body to pop right out of it and shout "Boo!"

When none did, Cody stepped forward. "I'll open it," he said. He inched his hand toward the lid.

"Oh no you don't!" I yelled, and grabbed his mitt. The little twerp had done this very same thing with those durn bees. He wasn't about to steal my thunder again. "*I'll* do it," I said. Cody smirked and shrugged and stepped back into the crowd.

Had I just been duped into opening a real live coffin, here in front of Cable's Mill?

Duped or not, I'd said I was going to open this here mystery casket. So I squinched up my nose as tight as I could to close off my sense of smell. No telling what a washed-up dead body might smell like. Geese, I bet. I turned my face over my shoulder, reached one hand out to the soggy box, and tried to flip open the lid with a twitch of my fingers.

I do things different. It helps to remind yourself of that when you're reaching into a box of death.

Now, what you don't know before a stray coffin washes up at your feet is that the lid to said coffin is heavy. Real heavy. So just a flip of the wrist didn't cut it. I soon found myself kneeling in the mud, jimmy-ing my fingers into the crack between the lid and the box. What was I *doing*, sticking my digits into heaven knows what? I took a deep breath and readied myself for what might be inside, just beyond my fingertips.

"One. Two. *Three!*" I heaved the pine lid open and leapt backwards faster than a cat with a stomped-on tail. The crowd sucked in a huge breath.

Empty!

The crowd let the breath go. Other than the pillowy, mud-stained velvet lining the inside, the coffin was empty. I'd never been so happy to see nothing in my whole life.

Beef guffawed and slapped me on the back. "Sure were lucky on that one. Guess you could say we mighta been up the creek without a paddle, har-har!"

Paddle?

And then I got the most wonderful, incredible idea. I sure could stand to be distracted, what with this park and Pop and all. And I knew just the way to do it. I jumped into the washed-up box and grabbed ahold of the sides.

"Gimme a shove, Beef," I yelled. "I'm going for a ride!"

Beef whooped. "Now thar's a dandy idea!" He placed his hands on the edge of the coffin and dug in the toes of his shoes, readying himself for a mighty push. "Hang on!"

"Wait!" Cody shrieked, sounding an awful lot like a girl. "I'm going, too."

"No!" I shouted, but it was too late. Cody had already hopped in and Beef had already pushed the coffin-turned-canoe into Abrams Creek by the time the word got off my lips.

The deep, cold, muddy water lifted us off the shore and hurled us down the creek, leaving the shouts of our neighbors behind. We spun, we bounced, we rocked, we teetered, we hollered—boy, did we holler! Cody knew more cuss words than I'd ever dreamed of! My insides felt like a big, fluttering moth, and my stomach was in my throat every time the coffin lifted, lifted, lifted . . . then peaked and toppled over a tall rapid, crashing back down to the muddy surface. I thought that coffin might splinter into a million tiny toothpicks, the way the creek'd pick us up and slam us back down again, next to all sorts of jagged rocks. But old Mr. McCauley was quite the craftsman, all right, because our makeshift canoe did just fine carrying us through those swollen rapids. It was, in fact, our own little luxury liner, what with the plush velvet lining cushioning the blows. A right comfortable coffin, it was.

I rode that old coffin like I was a cowgirl taming a wild bronco: hands waving, hair flapping, mouth whooping. It sure felt good having *something* under my control for once.

But then it occurred to me. We had no way to

stop this thing. The water was as powerful as a mule and as cold as ice; we couldn't just jump out and swim for shore. Cody must've thought the same thing because he started whimpering.

"How're we gonna get out of here, Autumn?" he shouted above the roar of the water.

I shrugged as best I could while gripping the sides of the coffin. The rocks got pointier and the drop-offs got steeper as we hurtled farther downstream. My throat clenched up, but I wasn't about to let on I was scared. "Guess we'll just have to ride this one out," I shouted back.

We kept rolling. And rushing. And rocking. And reeling. My stomach began to roll and reel even worse, and not just from the ride. My pop without a job! Riding a coffin through bumpy waters seemed like a premonition of some sort. A sign. Mama was always talking about signs and whatnot. I thought my stomach might spew like McCauley's old outhouse.

Then the creek spun us around and a wave of mud crashed into the coffin. The velvet cloth inside sucked up the soupy water and weighed us down.

"Bail it out!" I yelled. Cody and I were forced to turn loose of our white-knuckled grips on the sides of the coffin. We cupped our hands to scoop out the excess water. As we did, a surge of mud picked us up, up, up . . .

I do things different. It helps to remind yourself of that when you're sailing through the air toward a rocky riverbank.

I landed with a thud and a crash. What felt like a thousand lightning bolts jolted through my left arm, and the weight of the world seemed to crush me. I told myself to open my eyes.

Cody was lying on my chest, face to face. What was left of our canoe lay splintered on a massive boulder next to us.

"Get off me, creep!" I shoved Cody away, and that's when I noticed the gash on my arm. Cody looked like he might throw up at the sight of my blood. I actually smiled when I saw it—it was the first thing I'd seen in a week that wasn't mud-colored.

We panted like dogs for a moment. "Well, don't just sit there," I said, slowly standing. I felt real dizzy and sat back down.

"You okay?" Cody asked.

"Yeah," I said, pushing back the sleeve of my dress and looking at the cut a little closer. It was deep—deep enough to see white inside. Not good.

"Go get some dogwood bark, Cody."

"What?"

I smirked at my boating partner. "You know what a dogwood tree looks like, right?"

"Yeah. . . ."

"Peel the bark off and bring it to me. Understand?"

Cody scrambled around the area until he found a dogwood nearby, then started to scrape off the bark with his fingernail.

My arm was beginning to throb, and the sight of my own blood wasn't so welcome anymore. "Use a rock, Cody," I yelled to him. As he scraped, I spit onto my arm and washed out the cut as best I could.

He finally brought back a decent-sized pile of bark shavings. I wrung out my dress, then bit the hem and ripped a goodly bandage from it. I took the bark shavings, put them in the bandage, spit three or four times to work up a good paste, and wrapped the poultice around the cut.

"How'd you know how to do that?" Cody asked.

"Do what?"

"Do that with the bark?"

I shrugged. "Seen Mama do it a thousand times."

We sat there for a minute longer, looking at where we'd crashed. The floor of the forest curved up from the creek like we were in the bottom of a bowl. Boulders poked out of the earth, and clumps of azalea bushes bloomed fiery red in the cool shade of the tall pines and elms and oaks.

"Where do you 'spose we are?" Cody asked.

I looked around. "Townsend, maybe?" I groaned as I got to my feet. "Good luck finding your way back."

"What? Where're you going?"

I scanned the area again. Trees, trees, and more trees. Dang it!

"I dunno." I sank back down on the riverbank. I picked up a broad stone and winced as I chucked it sideways toward a wide spot in the water. We watched it hop five times across the surface before it disappeared. Cody gathered up stones, too. He pocketed some for his collection and tried to skip others. He's the worst rock skipper that ever lived.

Cody craned his neck all around like he was trying to memorize this place. I thought he might be formulating some heroic escape for himself and his injured leader, but instead he said, "The Great Smoky Mountains National Park. Has a nice ring to it, don'tcha think?"

The fool! He had no idea how lost we were. "Nope."

"Autumn Winifred Oliver!" Cody shouted, and leapt to his feet. He was so wound up it took me by surprise. I didn't even get the chance to frog him one for calling me by my full name. But he took a deep breath and kept going. "You move around as much as I have, you see lots. But nothing I've seen compares to east Tennessee."

He turned and threw his bony arms toward the sky. "If it weren't for the park, those lumber companies would strip this place bare. Take a look around, Autumn. This place is magic!" I couldn't help but look up and try to see this place with new eyes.

The trees twined their leafy fingers together, like they were tickling one another. Somewhere along the way it had stopped raining, and white sunlight poked through here and there in bright beams, spotting the ground with splashes of light and bouncing off the water in blinding bursts. The whole thing looked like one of Mama's lacy doilies. Birds chirped and water tinkled and leaves whooshed in near-perfect three-part harmony.

But still . . .

I shrugged. "How'm I supposed to know? I've never been anywhere else."

7

**I do things different.
It helps to remind
yourself of that
when you're filching
explosives from
the united States
government.**

We thought we'd best stay put and let ourselves be found. We sat there for the better part of the afternoon, and all the while Cody rambled on about stickball, poison ivy, banana cream pie, dungarees . . . I finally snapped like a dry twig.

"Cody! Don't you have any idea how lost we are?"

Cody's face went blank, but then a small grin crept across it. "Guess your hex worked, Autumn.

You told me to get lost, after all." I wanted to smack him.

I was getting jittery. It was looking like we'd have to sleep in the gully and hike out in the morning, but I wasn't about to let on that I was scared.

But after a few hours of staring at tree after towering tree, I couldn't help myself—my throat started to swell shut and my eyes got all teary and my arm started throbbing to beat all. How were we going to get out of here? We could try to follow the river back, I guess, but we must've traveled ten or eleven miles outside the Cove. By late afternoon the trees began to look less like they were tickling one another and more like they were clawing one another. I was *this close* to allowing a tear to plop out of my eye when a high-pitched *screeeeeeeeee* sliced through the air.

Cody sat up straight as an ironing board. "A saw!"

I nodded. It was a saw, all right. Now all we had to do was find it.

We tore off through the woods, scrambling up a steep slope toward the noisy saw. Trouble was, the sound stopped and started, stopped and started.

Cody and I must've looked like a coupla rats smelling out a hunk of cheese, what with us darting this way and that on our hunt.

"This'll teach you to bad-mouth those lumber companies, Cody!" I yelled in his direction. "Those saws are gonna save our hides! Cody! Cody?"

Finally I heard him yell, "Autumn, over here!"

I ran in the direction of his voice and found myself in a muddy clearing that was only about twenty feet wide, but it stretched for what must've been miles—as far as I could see from atop the bluff we'd just climbed. It might've been a road, but it was far wider than most of the dirt trails I'd ever seen.

A group of youngish men huddled round Cody like they'd just seen him walk across water to get to them, rather than just step out of the woods. They all wore uniforms—drab olive shirt, khaki pants, brown wool socks, muddy brown boots. The only thing that kept them from blending into the earth altogether was the shiny brass buttons on their collars. These weren't lumberjacks, no sir. A twig of a young man stepped forward, turned off his chain saw, and scowled at me. The name tag above his right breast pocket read "Jonathon Parker."

"What the . . . what're youse two doing here? Where'd youse come from? Is that blood?"

He pointed at my arm, and I looked down at myself. Wet, muddy, bloody—we looked like a coupla corpses stumbling out of these woods. Me, again the walking dead.

"Well, we been riding the rapids, you see. . . ." I pointed to the bottom of the gully, where the coffin still lay smashed on the rocks below.

"Is that a casket?" Jonathon's voice was funny, like he was honking through his nose while he talked. Like a . . . a *goose*! I disliked him immediately.

"Yessir. I mean, uh . . ." I hate it when I get all flustered. "We're from Cades Cove."

Jonathon scratched his chin like a much older man and slid his eyes at his crew. "The Cove, huh. I suppose youse need a lift home, then."

He jerked his head at the beat-up jalopy parked behind him in the mud. Cody nodded.

"Yessir," I said, and my heart skipped a beat. "Do you mean—in an automobile?"

Jonathon tossed back his head and laughed a wallop, and the other soldiers chimed in. "Do I mean in an *aw-tow-mow-beeele?*" He imitated me Southern-style in a way that really pinched my ears. "Of course I mean in an *aw-tow-mow-beeele!*" With that, he laughed a big hardy-har-har. I hoped he'd drop his chain saw on his foot.

"Well, get in," he said. Cody and I climbed aboard and perched atop several wooden crates in the backseat. It was cramped, but hey, it was an *automobile ride*!

The soldier hopped into the driver's seat and put on a real showy display starting up the old machine. He checked the starting levers three and then four times before fishing a key out of his pants pocket and unlocking the steering wheel. Then he finally stomped on a switch in the floorboard, and the auto roared to life. He shot a farewell salute to his crew, and we bounced and jostled down the muddy road, the ride so bumpy my teeth rattled around in my mouth.

The soldier seemed to loosen up now that he was away from his buddies. "Man oh man, am I ever glad to get out of there," he honked, wiping his brow. "Youse can only cut so many trees before youse go a little squirrelly, ya know? Ha! Squirrelly—get it? Ha!

"Name's Jonathon Parker," he continued,

tapping his name tag. His drab shirt hung from his bony shoulders like it was strung up by two hooks. He couldn't'a been older than nineteen.

"From Boston," he said. "Beantown. I gotta tell ya, kids, do I ever miss baked beans."

I hate it when people call me *kid*. "You can get beans here, mister," I said. Where'd this guy think he was, Mars?

"Yeah, but here they put sugar in them. Everybody knows you put molasses in baked beans. *Sugar!* In the tea, too. It's crazy. Man oh man."

Ooooo, this guy got my red up. But before I could ask him if he really drank his tea without sugar, we hit an enormous pothole. Cody bounced off the crate and hit his head on the roof of the auto, then landed back on the wooden box with a thud. He reached under him and rubbed his tailbone.

"Hey, mister?" he asked. "What'd you say was in these crates again?"

Jonathon shot a look into the rearview mirror, so all's I could see was his eyes. "I didn't say." And then it seemed like an eternity before he added: "It's dynamite."

I do things different. It helps to remind yourself of that when you're setting atop several tons of explosives.

"Dynamite?" I said. "What kinda crazy army detail are you on, anyways?"

Jonathon laughed. "I'm not in no army! I work for the CCC."

I felt my eyes narrow. "The CCC?"

"The Civilian Conservation Corps."

"I know what the CCC is." What, did he think we don't have schools around here, either?

"We're building a national park. This old junky road?" He swept his arm outside the auto at the mud below. "It'll be a nice, paved parkway once the CCC boys are done blasting our way through these scrubby old mountains. Man oh man!"

We'd hitched a ride with a *park builder*? I considered flinging myself from the auto, but the road whizzing below us soon turned from mud to rock, and when it did, I knew we were in real trouble. We were climbing Rich Mountain, and fast. To our left, the mountain rose steep as a wall straight into the clouds. To our right, it plunged down, down, down so sharp that we were riding next to treetops—*the tops of trees!* I could feel the vomit in my throat.

"Mister, slow down!" Cody managed to choke out.

Jonathon gargled a laugh. "No problem, kid! We're all right. Unless, of course, we hit something."

My heart was thumping harder than the Right Reverend Feezell thumps his Bible, so when I heard the second saw of the day, I thought it was the blood rushing from my head. We'd rounded the bend on the Cove Loop Road and were bumping and skidding along toward my old house. As we got closer, I knew for sure what I heard: hammers and saws and snapping wood and breaking glass. Then I saw it. A chain saw ripping through the roof over the dogtrot. Shingles and sawdust flying. A team of workers prying loose every clean, white board from the frame of our house.

My childhood home looked like a skeleton eaten away by a swarm of termites. Man-sized termites. With tools. And they all wore the same uniform our driver wore.

I couldn't help myself. "Wait!" I yelled. Jonathon slammed on the brakes, and we skidded in the mud, fishtailing past a huge boulder and coming to rest within inches of an ancient oak tree. Jonathon let loose a long, low whistle.

He turned and glared at me. "What the heck are youse thinking, yelling at someone who's hauling as much stick as we are?"

"What're they doing to that house?" I pointed to our once-beautiful home as the kitchen sink flew out a side window and landed in Mama's azalea bush.

"What?"

"What're they doing to that house?" I repeated above the racket of the chain saw. I watched as all the clean living that had once gone on inside our cozy home was loosed to the wilds.

Jonathon shrugged. "They're ripping it down," he yelled back. "We got orders to level anything that doesn't look rural enough for the national park. Guess they want to play up that whole hillbilly angle for the tourists."

Hillbilly? I felt almost dizzy, I was so angry. "They ain't ripping it down to put up a new hotel?"

Jonathon laughed. "Nah. There won't be any hotels inside park boundaries. No living quarters whatsoever.

"Nope. All these homes," Jonathon yelled, and he slung his wrist across the Cove, "they'll either be torn down or turned into tourist sites. The churches and the mill . . . they say Cades Cove'll be the best part of the park."

I was confused. Wasn't this stupid park supposed to *end* at Cades Cove? Weren't we going to rake in all those tourist dollars?

And what did Gramps know about this? He was a sneak and a schemer, all right, but this was beyond even him. No way would he sell out the whole Cove. I was madder than a snake with two heads at him and this park, but I didn't want him to lose his farm over it. Besides, Gramps was the greediest one of them all. If he couldn't open up a hotel . . .

But I didn't have time to mull over the thought of tourists gawking at the places where I'd prayed and slept and relieved myself, much less to consider where I might next rest my head, because right then the roof over the dogtrot collapsed with a massive crash. Just in time, too, because it spared me from having everyone hear my heart crash with it.

I asked Jonathon to drop us on the Cove Loop Road, a good mile or so downroad from Gramps's cabin.

That way, maybe I wouldn't catch such an earful from Mama about hitching a ride with a stranger. And too, I didn't want Katie laying eyes on a man in uniform.

The first thing Mama did when we got home that night was make a fuss over my arm. The next thing she did was make me pick a hickory twig for my whipping.

The first thing *I* did when I got home that night was hide the stick of dynamite I'd stolen from Jonathon Parker.

I do things different. It helps to remind yourself of that when you've got explosives stashed under the hem of your dress.

8

I do things different.
It helps to remind
yourself of that
when you're trying
to keep a secret
as big as a
national park.

The next day I was near sick while the picture of our collapsing house burned in my brain. I twiddled the stick of dynamite that lay hidden beneath my mattress, and mulled over who I should confide in.

Mama? No. No way could I tell Mama her house had been torn down. Mama loved that house, with its big, airy windows and high ceilings and plank wood floors. To Mama, a house is a home, not just a building.

Pop? No. It'd take too long to send word. Dang it! Why couldn't he be around like other dads?

Gramps? Next.

Katie? Katie . . .

Yeah. Katie!

"You must've heard him wrong, Autumn." Katie fluffed the pillow behind her back and reclined on the bed again. She waved a fan that said *Patterson's Funeral Home* in front of her flushed face and took a big gulp of water from the bucket I'd drawn, as I was still hauling all the water round here. Katie is on the plump side and wilts like a pansy in hot weather. After all the August rain, September had turned brutal hot. Katie had spent most of her recent days behind that paper fan. "Tell me again what he said."

"He said that there wouldn't be any hotels *inside* the park."

"But the Cove isn't inside the park."

"It is now."

"Well, that don't mean—"

I sucked in a deep breath. *Here goes.* "They tore our house down, Katie." I was surprised to hear my voice crack.

Katie sprang upright, and her shiny brown curls flopped forward over her broad shoulders. "They what? Who?"

I told her about the group of CCC boys stripping our house clean. I told her about the kitchen sink, the azalea bush, the dogtrot. I told her they'd be doing the same to every newish-looking house in the Cove.

She leapt up from the bed. Katie hadn't moved that fast in two weeks. She grabbed my hand so tight I thought my fingers might meld together.

"C'mon, let's find Gramps. That old coot has gone too far."

We found Gramps in the barn-turned-hotel. The next ten minutes of my life played out like I had some two-bit part in one of Miss Winstead's schoolhouse productions:

Gramps: "Come again?"

Katie: "I said this time you've crossed the line."

Gramps: *Cold, menacing stare.*

Me: "But—"

Katie: "Them CCC boys are tearing down all the Cove houses! My house—*Mama's house*—is gone, thanks to you and your silly park!"

Gramps: "Aw, they ain't tearin' down any houses."

Katie: "They are so!"

Gramps: "Says who?"

Katie: "Says Autumn!" *Finger in my direction.* "She saw them do it!"

Gramps: *Short, throaty grunt.* (Which, translated, meant, "That girl? She don't know her head from a hole in the ground.")

Me: "But—"

Katie: "If you don't believe her, go see for yourself."

Pause.

Gramps: "They's puttin' up a hotel."

Me: "But—"

Gramps: *Snap!* "Listen here, you two. You're lucky your mama ain't here to witness you tellin' these lies. Now, I'm sorry your pop's gonna be out of work, but that ain't no reason for you to go making up tales. If I hear another word about this from either one of you . . ." His icy glare shifted from Katie to me. "Well, let's just say the last few weeks of chores have been a real party compared to what they *could* be."

Gramps stomped out of the barn. I didn't even get to explain that *I* didn't think Gramps was mixed up in this. I didn't get in one stinking word.

Katie whipped around to me, her green eyes burning. "Autumn, don't you breathe a word of this to *anyone*, you hear? You know what kind of shame this'd bring on our family if folks knew they was losin' their homes because of Gramps's park? It's bad enough they're losin' all them lumber jobs." She rubbed her earlobe so hard it turned red.

"Nope, not a word. If you do . . ." She leaned in toward me, and I could smell sweat and talcum powder. "If you do, I'll tell Mama about that little bundle you've stashed under your mattress."

And then she stomped away, too. Now, how could she know where I chose to hide my explosives?

Katie and I trudged the three miles to school through the fields of sloppy mud, Katie working over that earlobe of hers the whole way.

"Now remember, not a word about this park, got it? I don't want to ruin the entire school year on the first day back." It was early September, one loooooooong week since my coffin ride. The longest week of my life. I might be the worst secret keeper in the whole world, but I'd managed to keep my mouth shut the entire week. But before me lay the true test for a reformed gossip: school. I thought I just might choke on this secret if I didn't turn it loose soon.

We approached the grove of oak trees under which our small white schoolhouse nestled. A group of kids hovered outside. Katie's big frame seemed to grow straighter, lighter. "Mable, wait!" she yelled, and ran off. I ducked inside the dank schoolhouse and plunked down on my bench. One row further back than last year. Better view out the window.

The scene out that window hadn't changed and wasn't likely to for, oh, the next hundred years or so. As everyone filed in and found this year's spot, a ratty gray squirrel chattered a song from his perch in an old oak: *I'm-outside-you're-inside. I'm-outside-you're-inside. I'm-outside-you're-inside.* Stupid squirrel.

We said the Lord's Prayer, and the first day of school got under way. I thought if I could twitch my knees fast enough, swing my feet high enough, sigh my breaths loud enough, this godforsaken day just might go faster. I was wrong. Crept, it did. I'd been sitting on that bench (which might as well've been made of sandpaper and bent nails, for all its comfort) for *years*. Okay, so three hours.

To pass time I made a list in my head of all the things that were mucked up right now. Mama calls it a "laundry list." I sure felt like I had been rubbed raw across a tin washboard. The list went something like this:

↔ Pop will lose his job.

↔ Gramps will lose his farm.

↔ Gramps is furious with me because he thinks I'm making up the bit about him losing his farm because my pop is losing his job.

↔ Katie is mad at Gramps because she's convinced he's sold us all out.

↔ No one knows about any of this, not even Mama. (Keeping a secret from Mama is about as easy as keeping a hound dog from sniffing out your trail.)

↔ Since Pop is losing his job, there's no reason for us to move to Knoxville. But we can't stay here, either, so . . .

↔ We're homeless.

↔ Everyone else I know will be homeless, too.

↔ I'm grounded, thanks to my coffin adventures with Cody.

↔ Cody is a known park supporter, and his loyalty is thereby in question.

↔ And oh, yeah . . . my very clever classmates keep pinching me, just to make sure I haven't up and died on them again.

". . . and that's how babies are made."

Cody stood at the front of the one-room school-house, feet crossed at the ankles, eyes on the dusty wooden floor. He swayed like he just might take a header, and his face burned like an ember. The rest of the forty-two faces in the class glowed, too, and those who could muster any bit of sound managed to spit out a giggle. Even the older kids—Katie and her gaggle of friends—were rapt. What had I missed?

Miss Winstead stood and smoothed her skirt. "Uh, thank you, Cody, for that extremely detailed report on the, ahem, reproductive system. I believe anyone in the class can tell you, however, that I asked if you knew anything about the *respiratory* system? Breathing?"

At the mention of breathing, the whole class exhaled. Shoulders shook and giggles turned to belly laughs. Even Cody managed a smile.

Miss Winstead pinched the place where the top of her nose and the bottom of her forehead meet. She does that a lot. "Class dismissed."

I scrambled out the door and down the schoolhouse steps to the group gathered under the oak to play Club Fist. Twig Ogle and the rest of the girls ran off to play Drop the Handkerchief, but I preferred my pastimes to be more rough-and-tumble. A good game of Club Fist should make me forget this dadblamed park for a while. But even as fast as I am, I was one of the last ones to the circle. Five fists stacked together already! But to beat all, the top thumb was hitched to none other than Tommy Bledsoe. I shrugged and grabbed ahold of his thumb as tight as I could. Cody stepped up and grabbed my thumb, making his fist the top of the club. Seven fists in all. Not a bad round.

Donnie Dunlap was it. He was a big oaf, but as soft as bread. Shouldn't be any problem hanging on to the club with him as odd man out.

"Take it off or knock it off, Cody?" Donnie asked him.

Cody sagged like a bag of flour. "Take it off, I guess." He let go of my thumb and stepped out of the ring.

"Dang it, Cody!" I said. "Don'tcha even want to try?"

Cody crinkled his forehead at me like I'd hurt his feelings or something. Jeez.

Donnie turned to me. "Autumn, take it off or knock it off?"

I shot Cody a bullet of a glance. "Knock it off."

Donnie licked his lips like he was studying how to remove my fingers from their clasp around Tommy Bledsoe's thumb. I steadied myself and tightened my grip.

"So, Autumn, tell us s'more about your coffin ride," Tommy said.

I smiled inside, not a little surprised that the request had been posed by my sworn archenemy.

"Well," I started, deciding to suck my teeth for effect, "I think we left off where I was just about to tackle a wild boar so's me and Cody wouldn't starve to death, when a gargantuan explosion shook the ground and drove the boar away."

Donnie stepped up and tried to pry my fingers open. I tightened my grip around Tommy's thumb.

"That's not how it happened," Cody said, crossing his arms across his chest.

Tommy and the rest of the Club Fist circle looked at Cody, then at me.

I panicked. Nobody ever called Gramps out like this!

"It was," I protested. "At least until we ran into that no-good bunch of park builders—"

"Boy howdy, that park!" Tommy interrupted. "My dad says that park'll be the best thing ever happened to Cades Cove. Says we may even have to start storing our money in a bank, we'll be so rich. Think I'll buy me a full-bred golden retriever with all that dough. How 'bout you, Donnie?"

Donnie shrugged but never looked away from my grip. "Well, I reckon I'd buy me a Smith and Wesson."

"I'm gonna get a John Deere tractor!"

"A new Chevy pickup!"

"A Kodak camera!"

Then Tommy Bledsoe smiled at me—*smiled!* "How 'bout you, Autumn? What'll you buy?"

I do things different. It helps to remind yourself of that when you're keeping a secret so big and so nasty it makes your skin itch.

It wasn't fair, holding on to a secret like this one. They needed to know they were about to lose everything. I could have just blurted it all out. *Cody* could've just blurted it all out. He had nothing to lose, being the new kid. But nah—he'd never do that. He was all for the stinking park.

In the background, Twig Ogle and the girls held hands and chanted over their handkerchief:

"There is so much good in the worst of us,
And so much bad in the best of us,
That it ill becomes any of us
To talk about the rest of us."

My grip on Tommy's thumb loosened, and Donnie slid his fingers under mine and pried my hand loose. "Aha!"

I suddenly felt all dizzy and sick. I shook my head. "A, uh, a . . . a *zeppelin*." I nodded. "Yeah, I'd buy me a zeppelin, all right."

"Wow!"

"Boy oh boy!"

"Just like the *Hindenburg*! Ain't she a beaut!"

9

**I do things different.
It helps to remind
yourself of that
when you suddenly
find that you're the
snake offering up
the forbidden apple.**

After my coffin adventure, Mama had decided that part of my punishment would be teaching me how to knit. So every Saturday morning, we'd gather up the supplies and Mama would proceed to snap at me for the next hour or so. I'd rather floss a bull's teeth than sit still for as long as it takes to knit a sample square. I drop more stitches than big fat Aunt Lydia drops cookie crumbs into her cleavage.

But one thing my knitting spells did let me do was puzzle how to get Gramps to believe me about this park mess. I'd tried to get him to hitch up his team and ride with me to our old house, but he'd have nothing of it. I figured Gramps'd find out in due time that I was right, that the Cove really would be inside the park, not bordering it, and that everyone would lose their homes because of it. That all his coaxing and sweet-talking and persuading our neighbors would leave him with naught. In a way, it served him right for not trusting his kin. Course, nobody deserved what I thought he was gonna get.

"And then you loop the thread around the needle—other way, Winnie. No—other way! And push it through the loop with the—no, honey. *Through* the loop. No. Here—like this . . ." I bet right about then Mama was regretting adding this chore to my list.

Cody burst into the cabin. He was still hanging around, even though I'd made it clear that he was now the enemy, him being for the park and all. But he didn't seem to mind.

"Excuse me, Miz Oliver," he said to Mama. "I saw Mr. Tipton on my way in. He wants Autumn to come right away."

Gramps wanted *me*? The stubborn coot hadn't ad-dressed me or Katie directly since Katie confronted him, and that had been two weeks ago. (Instead he'd say things like, "Martha, tell your girl she's to clean up that dog poo she's tracked in again." Mama just ignored all the ill feelings. She's not one to meddle.)

Mama nodded at me, so I followed Cody out to the yard. He showed me then that his fingers were crossed behind his back. "Sorry I lied to your mama, Autumn, but there's something I need to tell you and I knew she wouldn't let you out of the house for just me."

Once Cody told me what he'd overheard, I knew this was the way to show Gramps once and for all that *this* park was not *his* park. But I might have to dig out that stick of dynamite for the trip. Because we were headed to Chestnut Flats.

Getting Gramps to hitch up the wagon and take us for a ride was difficult, to say the least.

"I done told you, girl—no way I'm hitching up my team for you. You're still grounded," he grunted.

"Gramps," I finally flat out told him, "you're gonna want to see this."

Gramps huffed a big showy sigh, but to his credit, he pulled out his team and strung them up. I hoisted myself onto the wagon seat, and Cody hopped in the back. Gramps switched the lead horse and we took off at a handsome trot. I told him the briefest of directions so he wouldn't know that we were crossing the Cove, else he'd never go. The day glowed orangey yellow, and the air smelled like wet dirt after the big rain we'd had the night before. How is it that dirt smells so clean?

I'd never been to the Flats before. It was just eight miles from Gramps's cabin—about thirteen from our old house—in the southeast corner of the Cove. Rumor had it there were only about five or six families who lived there, but nobody knew for sure. Flats people kept to themselves—they married Flats people, had Flats babies, were buried in Flats cemeteries. But from what I'd heard, their living was anything but flat.

Folks in the Flats were known as far as Knoxville for their corn whiskey. Mama said it was a sin, the way they kept those moonshine stills running day and night. Mama said liquor and spirits and such had been outlawed for a reason, and she wasn't about to condone any lawbreaking in these parts (even though spirits had been legal again for a whole year now). Naturally, I was forbidden to go to the Flats.

But Mama was about to lose everything she knew. I figured she could turn the other cheek, since we were talking about the whole Cove losing the roofs over their heads, right? Besides, I was already grounded. So I touched the stick of dynamite tied to my leg and bit my tongue to keep quiet.

It was getting late in the day. The sun skimmed the mountaintops, throwing long, creepy shadows across the floor of the Cove. Gramps grew fidgety as we steered him toward the Flats.

Soon Cody pointed at a cluster of clapboard houses down the way. "Over there." A shiny black Ford sat in front of the shack he pointed to. ("Shack" was putting it kindly. I'd built treehouses that looked sturdier than that lean-to.)

"The Flats?" Gramps yanked the reins taut and we came to a halt about a half mile up the road. "You gone crazy?" He looked at me as he said this.

"Gramps, Cody overheard his uncle say to a CCC boy that he's got some business to conduct out here. I think you ought to be in on it."

Gramps shook his head. "I don't need in on any kind of business in the Flats. See no evil, hear no evil. Got it?"

I saw it flash across his face just then: Gramps thought the colonel was here to buy moonshine.

"Gramps, this ain't about moonshine!" I said, maybe a little too loud. But I was getting real hot with him not listening to me. "It's about the park."

"Colonel got no park business here," Gramps said, shaking his head and readying the reins. "Nope, let's just head on home."

I studied my gramps. Craggy old face, graying hair—he looked older than most fellas his age. Maybe the long string of failed get-rich schemes had taken a bigger toll than I knew. He really seemed to need this park, for more than just the money. He seemed to need a win.

"With all due respect, sir," Cody said, and cleared his throat. "Adam and Eve had a chance to stay in paradise, but they were dumb and they ignored all the warnings and they blew it."

I couldn't believe my ears! Here was this scrawny city kid sassing my granddad, telling him he was too dumb to see the signs. I braced myself for Gramps to spin around and whup him one. I know I would've. But instead, Gramps just sat there, shaking his head.

And this from the same kid who, just days ago, wouldn't shut his trap about the Cove being all magical and whatnot. That the park would be about the best thing that'd ever happened to this place. I couldn't stand it any longer. "Cody—are you for this stinking park or against it?"

Cody shrugged. "Let's just say I never saw a thing that lived up to its promises."

At that, Gramps seemed to wake up. He squared his shoulders and locked his jaw. "Let's go get us some knowledge of good and evil."

Gramps halted the wagon and sauntered up to the shack like he visited the Flats every Tuesday. A trickle of smoke rose up from the backyard. A sickening sweet smell, like burning molasses, smacked us in the face.

"Moonshine," I whispered to Cody. He nodded like he knew that already.

Gramps circled past the colonel's car and round the house. "George? You here, Burchfield?" How Gramps knew who lived here, I didn't know.

Then we saw it: a real moonshine still! On one end, a huge vat shaped like a potbelly stove sat over a small fire. Moonshine ran through rusty pipes and poured out into a barrel in a steady, water-clear stream. The whole thing burped and fizzed and stank to high heaven.

Screeeeee—blam! A screen door on the backside of the house squealed open, then banged shut.

A giant hulk of a man stepped outside and scanned the yard. He had to crane his neck all the way round to see us thanks to a puffy pink scar that sealed his left eye shut. He was bald and his head had a pointy shape to it, like a big acorn. He spat a long brown stream and swung a shotgun round to greet us.

I do things different. It helps to remind yourself of that when you're staring down the wrong end of a Smith and Wesson.

"Tom Tipton?" Pointy George swung the shotgun up over his shoulder. He smiled, which made his scar all crinkly. "You look worse'n a two-week-old cow pie on a hot summer day."

Gramps huffed but smiled. "Feel that good, too, Burchfield."

Screeeeee—blam! The infernal screen door opened and shut again, this time turning out Colonel Chapman. His eyes twinkled, but I couldn't tell if it was a flash of delight or disgust.

"Well, if this ain't some coincidence! The colonel here was just tellin' Momma and me"—Pointy George jerked his head toward a dried-up crabapple of a woman hovering near the door—"that you been workin' on some national park. Tellin' folks to lend their support, I hear."

"That is true."

I couldn't take my eyes off Pointy's momma. She scurried back and forth across the kitchen, hauling bags of cornmeal that must've weighed fifty pounds each. But she carried a huge, silvery butcher knife in her tiny fist the entire time.

"So it's true you're gonna sell your land and move out of the Cove? 'Cause I told the colonel here—" Pointy clasped a massive arm around the colonel, squeezing the shotgun between the two of them. "I told him they's no way Tom Tipton's sellin' his family land, no sir. Not a stubborn mule like Tipton."

The colonel looked pretty calm for a man with a shotgun under his chin, but he was white as flour. Pointy's momma had stopped hauling the bags of cornmeal and had begun stabbing open the bags with the butcher knife. She grunted each time she gutted a bag: "Huuun-*unh*!"

"I ain't sellin', Burchfield," Gramps said. "Sellin' wasn't part of the deal. Right, colonel?" Gramps fixed his eyes on the colonel like a hunter lines up a shot in his crosshairs.

"Huuun-*unh*!"

Colonel Chapman shrugged Pointy off his shoulders and moved toward his nephew. "Cody? May I ask what you're doing here?"

Gramps stepped between the two of them. "Boy's with me. Now, what's this about sellin' off my land?"

"Huuun-*unh*!"

The colonel's face drew into straight, flat lines. "I came here to offer Mr. Burchfield a fair price for his property." Pointy George huffed and his scar turned bright pink.

"A fair price, just like the offer you're going to get, Mr. Tipton," the colonel said.

"Sellin' wasn't part of the deal," Gramps repeated. If he was a snake, he'd'a hissed it.

"The deal has changed, Mr. Tipton."

"This is the first I'm hearing about this, Colonel." Gramps was as staid and stolid as the ring of mountains around us, but for some reason, a wave of pity washed over me as I watched him fight for his farm. I hated it. I didn't want to feel pity for him. He wouldn't want it, neither.

"Huuun-*unh*!"

"C'mon, Tom," the colonel said, and my ears curled at this fella calling my gramps by his familiar name. "You really think those tourists want to bunk up with a bunch of strangers?" He motioned to Pointy's shack, as if this box represented all the houses in the Cove.

"That's how it's done in the Cove."

"That's not how it's done anywhere else in the world."

The colonel and Gramps stared each other down like two crouched cats. The colonel finally cracked. "Tom, we needed your help in selling the idea of a national park to your neighbors." *Who is this "we"? I wondered.* "After all, do you really think they would've listened to someone like myself?" He stretched his arms out, and his razor-sharp suit and shiny shoes made his point for him.

"Tom, you helped us, and we thank you for fulfilling your civic duty. But the time has come for the Cove to enter a new age. I would think you'd be excited about that opportunity."

"I won't sell."

"Huuun-*unh*!"

The colonel laughed, and I realized it was the first time I'd seen him look truly happy. "Tom. You're dealing with the federal government here. You don't have a choice."

The wound on my arm throbbed, the dynamite on

my leg itched, and I wanted to jump right out of my skin, I was so hot.

"Off." Pointy George jabbed his finger toward the road.

"Pardon?" Colonel Chapman whirled to face Pointy. The colonel's face was all smiley on one side, like this situation didn't call for a full-face smile.

"Off my land." Pointy George never blinked his one good eye.

The colonel sighed real showy. "Oh, George. Don't you see? It's *my* land." With a sweep of his wrist, he laid claim to the whole Cove.

"Not yet it ain't," Pointy said. "Off. My. Land."

Colonel Chapman twisted his neck real slow, like he was about to say something else. But instead he rounded the house, folded himself inside his auto, and drove away, the tires flinging mud and clumps of dirt behind them.

Gramps's craggy face trapped the shadows of late afternoon, and he looked like a crumpled-up wad of paper. At last he believed me. But now I felt lower than a snake's belly.

10

I do things different.
It helps to remind
yourself of that
when Uncle Sam
himself forces you
to say uncle.

It took but a half day's sunlight for word to make its way
to all the neighbors. Gramps sprang into action like a
mountain lion. He posted signs all over the Cove:

Feel Cheated? Meet at the
Schoolhouse Friday Next
at Sundown to Discuss
"Our" National Park!!!

Pop heard about the meeting through a friend of
Jeremiah Butler's, and sent word back that he'd be

there. He hitched a ride in on a lumber truck specially for it. I waited for him on the front porch, rocking and picking at the scab on my arm. When I saw his blond head come across that swinging bridge, it was like watching the sun rise.

"Pop!" I leapt off the porch and was inside his mighty hug in three bounds. He smelled like sweat and coal smoke, and a razor hadn't touched his jaw in weeks. "That you in there, Pop?" I giggled.

Pop swung me around until I was dizzy. "Autumn! How's my favorite season?" I grinned to beat all.

I wanted to seem more grown-up for my pop, so I answered as Mama would: "Living and breathing, so I guess I can't complain."

Pop laughed. "Well, I hear we're awfully lucky 'bout that, now, aren't we? Not everyone gets to hear their own death tolls ring."

"Pop!" I got in one good tickle before Mama and Katie came spilling out of the cabin and tackled us. For a minute I forgot all about scabs and dynamite and moonshine stills and parks. The four of us hugging together were far stronger than any old ring of mountains.

Pop always said that Mama had the steadiest hand of any person he knew. Should've been a sharpshooter, he says. 'Cause of that, Mama has always been the one to take the straight razor to Pop's whiskers. He wanted to clean up before the big meeting, so they set everything up at Gramps's kitchen table.

The lanterns glowed warm yellow. Pop leaned back in a kitchen chair, the shaving bowl and razor on the table, a steamy cloth nearby to wipe away the excess soap. The only sound in the room was the *skritch, skritch* of Mama dragging the razor up Pop's neck, across his cheek. She worked so gently, so lovingly, that my chest like near squeezed shut thinking they were living so far apart.

I'd seen Mama shave Pop's beard a thousand or so times before, and normally it don't warrant a family gathering. But it'd been so long since we'd seen Pop, both Katie and I pulled up our own chairs at the table.

"So our house—it's completely gone, Autumn?" Pop asked, looking at me out of the corner of his eye while tilted back in the chair.

"Yessir. I'd imagine it is now."

Pop clicked his tongue. Mama swiped the blade clean against her apron and lowered it again to his throat. *Skritch.*

"Darn shame. Your daddy had a really good idea with that park, Martha." Mama nodded and pulled the razor near his ears. Tears puddled in her brown eyes. It looked to me like she was a whole lot sadder about losing the park than she had been about Pop losing his job. Come to think of it, Mama had been dragging around ever since she found out about this park mess.

"A really good idea," Pop repeated. He swiped at a poof of soap on his earlobe. "Could've been something big for folks around here. Could've been big for *us*. I sure would've liked to sell some of our artwork to all them tourists. Right, Autumn?" He started to nod. Mama gently swatted him with the rag and he steadied his bobbing head beneath the sharp razor.

My stomach like near flipped over. Sell artwork! I didn't know Pop had planned on that. That sure would've been fun, all right. I felt flat as a griddle cake now that I knew I'd lost that, too. That *we'd* lost that. Me and Mama and Pop and Katie. I guessed Mama had known this was the plan all along. Otherwise she would've been a lot worse off back when she found out Pop was losing his job at the lumber company.

"Daddy, what—" But before Katie could get any further, Mama shot her the hush-up look. Mama'd already warned Katie and me: no questions about the park. Not today. Pop would be too tired, and today was about family. It was about the hardest rule I'd ever had to follow.

Pop knew the rules, too, but he had to get in his say. "It's a shame those park builders had to do business that way."

Mama nudged him and offered up one of Katie's jeweled mirrors so he could examine her handiwork. He jutted his chin in the air and checked himself at all angles. The puffy purple circles under his eyes showed more now that his beard was gone. He skimmed his large, callused fingers over his clean, fresh face. There was nary a nick on his whole mug.

"Yep. Trust just ain't what it used to be."

That Friday evening, I'd just returned home from school when we circled around and went right back. Like near every landowner in the Cove showed up at the schoolhouse—even Pointy George and his crabapple momma filed in. Us kids weren't allowed inside, on account of no room. So while the grown-ups were getting situated inside, I circled round the back of the schoolhouse and pried open a section of latticework that sealed off the crawl space below the school. As I ducked inside, a spiderweb welcomed my face with a gluey hug.

A dozen or so kids crept in after me, all crouching in the narrow space. Katie came with us, though she probably could've sat with the adults. At first I thought she'd followed us 'cause Jackson Tucker had come with us kids, too, but then she settled in next to me.

Tough, gangly weeds sprouted in the dust, and the rustle of furry things in dark corners drew us kids in close. Donnie Dunlap had a tin of black licorice, and he silently doled out helpings to everyone huddled below the school.

Footsteps and the scraping of chair legs on wooden floors were the only sounds coming from above. It was right uncomfortable, all those yakky grown-ups thrown together and nary a one of them speaking a word. Finally, I heard Gramps clear his throat.

"Folks, we all know why we're here. I'm open to suggestions on how to keep this park off our land."

There was an eternity of silence before somebody—it might've been Uncle John Too—said, "Can't we file a lawsuit or something?"

Somebody shouted, "Lawsuit! Who has money to pay for lawyers?"

Somebody else: "I knowed this park was too good to be true. I knowed it, and none of y'all listened to me!"

Then another voice said, "When's all this supposed to happen? How much time we got?"

"Nobody knows. We might get to live out our lives here, or we might get kicked out next week. We're spitting into the wind—who knows which way it'll fly."

Someone else chimed in, "Seems to me like this is a right good time to sell. Crops don't bring near enough cash these days to keep my family fed. I don't mind getting fair wages for my land, no sir. I hear they's work in Knoxville and Maryville. Nope, I plan on taking the first offer."

"Traitor!" somebody yelled. "We got to fight this united. If one person sells, we're all out!"

"That's no way to talk to your neighbor!"

"So you're just gonna leave your great-granddaddy's land, are you?"

"For the right price."

"For the right price you'd hitchhike nekked to Gatlinburg!"

"Enough!" A chair scraped across the floor. "Okay, folks, listen here."

Pop! Here it comes: the answer.

"What I'm gonna say ain't gonna sit well with some of y'all. Y'all are sitting on some real valuable property. If it ain't the park gonna buy you out, the lumber companies will. And you ain't seen nothing sadder than a mountain stripped bare of all its trees. Trust me on that.

"I've torn apart whole communities limb by limb," he continued. His voice wavered with a hint of an apology behind it. "When there ain't trees to protect a community, to give it shade and shelter, there ain't nothin' left. With no trees, the rain'll either pool into puddles, or wash all the good topsoil into the rivers. Nothin' but scrubby weeds and bushes can take root in that kind of mess. And no river is the same after it's been clogged up with all that mud. I can't bear to think of the Cove slashed down like that. Nope, if it wasn't for the mouths I gotta feed, I would never work a job like this. Never."

If anyone else felt like me at that moment, then they also felt like pieces of day-old fruit suspended in a drippy Jell-O mold. Katie took my hand.

Pop grunted, and the strength in his voice returned. "So if we do have to sell out to the park—which it sure sounds like we do—well, then, we might lose a few buildings here and there. But I'd say we'd all agree that's better than stripping bare our land. Let's thank heaven our land was spared the saw."

"Exactly!" I heard Gramps leap forward. "I know everybody here thinks I wanted this park for the money. Chasing rainbows, right, Lydia?"

I could just imagine big fat Aunt Lydia's face growing red up there.

"Don't get me wrong—the money would've been nice." Gramps managed a huff of a laugh. "But I don't have to tell you what a mess those lumber companies are making. Mud washing down the mountains, pooling in our fields and destroying our crops. And Marvin"—Gramps stomped his foot at Mr. Proffitt for emphasis—"that eight-foot bear that came wandering round your homestead? It's likely his home was destroyed by loggers, right?"

"You knowed it."

"A park seemed like the perfect resolve: the loggers would stop logging, we could make a little extra money on the side . . ."

His voice trailed off, and all the shuffling and murmuring and whispering halted.

Gramps coughed. "Listen, folks, I—" Even from underneath the dusty floorboards, I heard the catch in his throat.

"I'm sorry. Dang it. I am truly sorry about getting us into this mess."

I knew from where I crouched that my gramps had tears in his eyes. I'd never seen him cry. I wasn't really seeing him cry now, but knowing he was up there teary-eyed in front of all those folks made my throat clench up and the tip of my nose tingle.

Katie, crouched next to me, was the first person to let loose a big, heaving sob. She cried like those sobs of hers just might cleanse us of all these wrongdoings. I hugged her close. She smelled like honeysuckle in the springtime.

11

**I do things different.
It helps to remind
yourself of that when
the same horrible
ditty plays in your
head over and over
and over again.**

Same song.
Second verse.
Sing it over.
Jes' like the first.

I say that because most times in the Cove, a
Monday is a Tuesday is a Wednesday. Oh, sure, there's
the occasional spelling bee here and the rare singing
school there. But for the most part, it's all likeness. No
difference. But now, something's different every day,

and I can't say I cotton to it, even as much as I enjoy doing things different. So I think we were all glad to see the Syrup Soppin' Festival roll around. This year, folks in the Cove needed a festival like this to take their minds off their park woes, if only for a day or two.

Do I ever love to sop some syrup! Every second weekend in October, folks from all over the Cove—all thirty families, minus the Flats folks, who never come to such gatherings—meet up at the schoolhouse with their sorghum harvest in tow. Every last stalk gets fed between a contraption with two rollers. The contraption mashes those crisp green reeds, and eventually they ooze syrup. The juice dumps into Beef Jackson's huge iron pan. Donnie Dunlap's daddy hitches up his team of mules, and the old nags march round and round the pan. It's up to all us kids to keep the fire stoked and the pan stirred, lest the syrup freeze up or bloop over.

But the best part is the music—whew! Can those old boys put some pepper in it! Uncle John and Uncle John Too bring out the banjo and the mandolin, and Marvin McBroom and his brothers bring out the fiddles, and before you know it, we got ourselves a real frolickin'. (Especially when somebody—I won't say who, Gramps!—brings out the happy juice.) Folks even start dancin'. Mama says such twistifications are the devil's work, but even she's been known to tap a toe or two at the Syrup Soppin' Festival.

And because the making of syrup is a round-the-clock effort, everybody in the Cove pitches tents right there on the school grounds, and everybody takes turns manning their watch. Me, I drew the four a.m. detail. So naturally I decided it would be wiser to stay up all night, lest I oversleep.

Yeah, this Syrup Soppin' Festival couldn't have come at a better time. If a fix to our woes was out there, it was sure to make itself known at a festival like this.

I wandered the campsite solo. Long about midnight, the kids started playing Roses Are Red, Violets Are Blue. It only took one verse—

Autumn's father went to borrow a chair,
When he got there, Cody was hugging his dear.
Cody's mother went to borrow a pan,
When she got there, Autumn was hugging her man.

—before I got up and left. Buncha hooligans!

I went to see if Katie needed a hand on her shift,

but she sure seemed to have it under control, what with that new Peter Lockland fella who was visiting from the Sugarlands doing all the fire stoking and pot stirring for her. Jeez! That girl and her want of a beau.

So I went to sit with Mama and the other hens. All the biddies were prepping this winter's leather britches beans, stringing snap beans onto lengths of yarn. I took to cutting up the yarn for them.

"And so now those park officials are sayin' that if we're lucky, they'll let us lease back our land from the government. Lease it!" big fat Aunt Lydia bellowed. "Imagine paying rent to live in a house you been in your whole life. Confounded park!"

Mama cleared her throat and jerked her head toward me. "Lydia . . . little pitchers . . ."

Ain't it funny how grown-ups think if they don't tell you something directly, you'll never find out the secret? "Don't worry, Mama. I know all about it."

Even by firelight, I could see Mama raise her eyebrows at me. What, did she think I hadn't figured out what was going on by now? Jeez, sometimes parents don't give you any credit. So I proved myself.

"That park is buying everyone out and forcing them out of the Cove. The colonel? He lied when he said everyone could stay here and get rich. There's no fortune to be had. And doesn't he work for the president and all those government officials? I say, confounded *government*."

Now, let me stop right here for a second. On any given night in the Cove, it's a noisy thing, darkness. There's leaves rustling and cows bleating and water rushing and crickets chirping. But when you cuss the United States government—the very government that our Cove grandfathers stayed loyal to, even while living in a Confederate state during the Civil War—I swannee, every single noise stopped right then, so one and all could hear my truths echo off these dadblamed mountains.

Out of the darkness came a noise I never thought I'd welcome: the sound of teeth-sucking.

"Girl's half right," Gramps said. "But the real truth? Cove is *cursed*. Cursed by a Cherokee Indian chief."

Ttttttthhhhhhuuuuuussssssssuuuuupppppp!

Yep, that teeth sucking sounded like sweet, sorrowful fiddle music about now. Gramps hitched up his overalls with his thumbs. At the mention of the word *curse*, Mama bowed her head and shot off a short prayer of forgiveness for her heathen daddy.

"Cursed by Chief Kade himself. Yep, that old chief cursed the land that was named for his very soul. He'd'a rather seen it fall to ruin than end up in the hands of us settlers.

"Legend has it," he kept on, though nobody asked him to, "that the ruckus made from the first blow of the forge hammer in Cades Cove drove all the wolves away. The Cherokee thought the *wáya*— that's Cherokee for 'wolf,' you know—was some sort of revered watchdog. Anything that would scare them away was surely gonna take away their land, too."

"A forge hammer took their land?" I asked.

Gramps snapped his fingers at me. "Progress, girl! Progress! Them Cherokee Indians wanted nothing to do with saws and shotguns. Nope, give them a hatchet and some blow darts any day. They made settling up the land round these parts mighty difficult, I recall hearing. That's why they's asked to leave."

I looked from Gramps to Mama and the hens and back to Gramps. No one seemed to want to ask the next question, so I shook off the scolding I'd gotten last go-round and asked away.

"They got asked to leave?"

Even in the moonlight, I could see Gramps pull his mouth to one side of his face. "Yep. 'Bout a hundred years ago. Government came and rounded 'em all up and sent 'em to Oklahoma."

Danged if silence didn't smother us all again. Mama smoothed her dress across her lap. The other hens sat still as stumps. Even big fat Aunt Lydia was quiet. Because the same thing was happening to us right now. It was the same song, second verse. It was all too familiar.

"Confounded government." This time it was from Gramps.

The quilt in Mama's lap pooled around her feet. I lifted a corner of it and snuggled underneath. I didn't want to ask no more questions. I was all asked out. I looked up at the hundreds of stars that hung above and picked out Orion. Three stars in his belt. It was the last thing I remember seeing, until . . .

"Girl? Girl, wake up!" It was Gramps, shaking me out of a deep slumber. "Girl, what time's your shift?"

My eyes fluttered open. The outline of dawn peeked around Gramps's gray head like a halo. It was how I imagined a cranky angel would look. "Um—four a.m.?"

"Cripes, girl, get up!" He yanked me to my feet. "It's near five. Syrup's done froze up. Let's go!"

One thing about Autumn Winifred Oliver—rarely do I see fit to cry over such mishaps. Salt's expensive. Why waste it in tears?

But boy, was I ever close to spilling some salt when I saw the mess of goo setting in Beef's iron pan. The fire had long since burnt out, so the syrup'd turned cold and thick. The mules were braying and stomping and snorting, trying with all their fool hearts to stir up this glue. My bottom lip quivered.

"Now's not the time for blubbering," Gramps said, and patted me on the back. "Wait right here. And unhitch those durned mules before they wake somebody up."

I scampered around the vat and turned the mules loose. One of them dropped to her knees and fell dead asleep. I felt like doing the same, minus the asleep part. I'd ruined all my neighbors' syrup for the whole year! They'd have my hide!

I stoked the fire under the vat and got it back to a gentle roar. Gramps returned, hauling four huge ceramic jugs—one in each hand, one in each armpit. He didn't even look at me before he uncorked the first jug and poured it in. The stench hit me like I had bees up my nose. Whiskey!

"Gramps!" I whispered. "Where'd you get—"

"Hush, girl!" he whispered back. He jutted his chin toward one of the jugs he'd dropped next to the vat. "Pour it in."

I uncorked the jug, and listened to the *glub-glub-glub* of five gallons of whiskey being dumped into the Cove's syrup supply. I thought the smell alone would get me drunk. "Couldn't we just try—"

"Water's not quick enough." Gramps shook his head. "We gotta loosen the tug before Beef gets here for the next shift. Nope, gotta use whiskey. This'll loosen her up."

And then something amazing happened: Gramps laughed. Not just a snort. Not just a guffaw. A full-out belly laugh.

"This stuff'll loosen *anything* up!" he finally managed to spit out. He wiped a tear from his left eye.

Then it hit me. The fear and sadness and guilt I felt by letting down my neighbors over a silly batch of syrup must be what Gramps felt about this park. Every day. Times a hundred.

"What're you two doing?"

The voice was too deep, too gravelly for me to recognize. I froze up like the syrup in the pan below me. I didn't dare turn to see who was riding us. Then I heard giggling.

"Boy, are we ever glad to see you," Gramps said. Out of the corner of my eye, I saw him hand over a ceramic jug. "Pour it in."

Cody! I could swat him one for sneaking up on us like that, pretending to be all uppity. I turned loose the breath I'd been holding and smiled at him.

I had just clicked the last hitch and smacked the lead mule on the rump to start the team marching when I heard Beef whistling a hearty good morning.

"Hiya there, Autumn!" he said, and thumped me on the back. "Mr. Tipton." He nodded to Gramps, who was throwing a burlap sack over four empty ceramic jugs. "Cody."

Gramps straightened and grinned a too-large grin at Beef, and I just knew we'd been caught. "Mornin', Beef. Whyn't you try some syrup?"

I shot a look of fury at Gramps—that whiskey hadn't had time to blend in yet! But sure enough, Beef stuck out his meaty forefinger and dipped it right in.

"Don't mind if I do," he said, and put a glob of shiny yellow syrup on his big tongue.

Okay, so being drug out behind a team of wild horses wasn't how I'd originally pictured leaving the Cove, but that was how it would happen now that Beef had tasted our dirty little secret, right?

But instead he smacked his fat lips. "Mmmmm! This may be the best batch yet—even better than the infamous batch of 'twenty-eight!"

Gramps clamped a hand around Beef's shoulder. "I think folks'll be real happy with this batch." He winked at me. "*Real* happy."

I do things different. It helps to remind yourself of that when you're about to slip the whole town a batch of devil's syrup.

12

**I do things different.
It helps to remind yourself of
that when you're
fending off the circling,
swooping vultures.**

Nobody seemed to notice the funny batch of syrup they'd carted home from the Syrup Soppin' Festival the week before, and I kept mum about sullying all my neighbors. But ever since I'd felt that letting-everyone-down noose tighten around my neck, I knew I had to help bail Gramps out of this park mess.

How Autumn Winifred Oliver can Stop the National Park:

- ~~Poison the water supply.~~
- ~~Burn all trees and crops.~~
- ~~Kidnap Col. Chapman. (Is it still kidnapping when it's a grown up?)~~
- ~~Flood the cove (plus there'll be a big new lake).~~
- ~~Destroy the road into the cove.~~
- ~~Build great big wall around cove (Cody says it worked for China).~~
- ~~Spread rumor of giant fire ants.~~
- ~~Spread giant fire ants?~~
- ~~There's always that stick of dynamite . . .~~
- Just not move?

Every idea I had seemed too big or too dumb or it would end up ruining the Cove, which is what I was trying to stop in the first place. But "Just not move" might be an option. I mean, what could they do to us—drag us out by our shirt collars? Ha! I'd like to see one of those CCC boys try to put a hand on Gramps's neck. They'd be worm food faster than a fly mop whups a housefly.

But while I pictured us camping out with our shotguns and waiting for some greasy park pushers to force us off our land, I decided to take a different tack. I penned a letter in my fanciest script and threw in the biggest words I knew so he'd take me serious:

October 23, 1934

Dear Mr. Rockefeller sir,

My name is Autumn Winifred Oliver, and I habitate in Cades Cove, Tennessee. It is my understanding that you, Mr. Rockefeller, have donated a gargantuan sum of dollars for the development of the Great Smoky Mountains National Park. I thought you should know the God's honest truth about said park. Said park will leave myself and my kinfolk without homesteads. If you could see fit to cease all donating until this mess gets straightened out, I would truly appreciate your kindfulness.

Sincerely and au revoir,

Autumn Winifred Oliver

Cades Cove, Tennessee

P.S. Au revoir is French. It means "goodbye." My teacher, Miss Winstead, says even people from as far away as France will visit this park, so she's taught us how to say hello and goodbye. But I don't know

why, 'cause we won't be here to say diddly-squat to any Frenchman.
P.P.S. "Hello" is bonjour

I passed the letter along through Jeremiah Butler's rolling store, with three cents for the post. I half expected Jeremiah to give me a ribbing when he saw the address, but he just tossed the letter on a heap of mail.

"And, oh, I'm real sorry 'bout your friend's mama," Jeremiah said as he hopped into his truck.

"What?"

"Your friend Cody." Jeremiah slung his elbow out the window and shook his head slow. "Got a telegram 'bout his mama yesterday."

A telegram? A telegram means only one thing: death. "You sure?"

"Yeah." Jeremiah clicked his tongue. "Folks say he'll just stay put with Matilda."

"Yeah," I murmured. I felt sick. "Stay put."

The chickens in the coop atop the cab of the truck squawked and flapped as Jeremiah drove away.

Cody said nary a word about his telegram the next day at school. So I didn't say nothing, either. That day passed, and then the next. Mama and Katie both asked me about it, but I didn't know anything more than what they'd gathered through Cove gossip. A few more days passed, and then it would've been downright awkward to say something to him. And so I said nothing.

I'd hoped things might settle down for a while so I could resume my normalities: school, chores, fishing. But that was not to be.

"You feelin' okay, child?" Mama laid the back of her hand against my forehead. "It ain't like you to forgo a second helping of flapjacks."

My stomach lurched right there at the breakfast table. I couldn't help feeling like every time I gobbled up a forkful of syrup-coated flapjacks, I was getting tipsy. I tasted nothing but hooch.

But that syrup wasn't the only thing making my belly ache. The park'd bought out five more families and torn down three more houses. Plus, folks in the Cove found it harder and harder to move their crops at market. Might've just been this depression, but rumors started that the government had put a block on our crops to drive us out of our homes, like you'd build a fire to smoke a nest of chimney swifts out of a chimney. Every time Katie and me asked, "Where will we go? What will Pop do for work? What will happen to Gramps?" Mama would just shrug and tell us that the Lord will provide. It didn't sound like a foolproof plan to me.

Mama hovered over me, waiting for me to explain my lack of appetite. I made up an excuse real quick. "Just nervous for Peter's visit, I suppose," I said, and tried not to roll my eyes.

Katie lit up like a lantern. "Oh, when Peter Lockland shucked that ear of corn and it was *red*? I always thought that tradition was silly, letting someone who shucks an ear of red corn pick someone to kiss," she said with a giggle. "But now I see. It's so special, red corn. Red corn don't happen along every day. Why, he could've picked any girl there to kiss, couldn't he, Mama?"

Mama smiled and nodded and drizzled some sinful syrup over her breakfast, like she was baptizing it in the name of all things depraved. Gramps watched her out of the corner of his eye, and I swannee the old geezer almost choked on his sausage link.

"But he picked me!" Katie crossed to the window in grand fashion, leaned out of it, and breathed in a lungful of air. "Me! Oh, who knew that I'd find my true love at a syrup festival? Who, indeed?"

Jeez! Katie'd been talking like this all week, ever since her first kiss. Mama says I'll talk like that, too, whenever I get kissed. In which case I can do without.

"And now he's requested a visit. A *visit!*" She reached under her skirt and pulled a crumpled letter from 'neath her garter.

" 'Dear Kathryn,' " she read, then looked up. "Did you hear that? *Kathryn!*"

Had I heard it? At least a hundred times, I'd guess.

" 'I reckon I'd fancy callin' on you,' " Katie continued reading. " 'If your folks don't mind, that is. Suppose I'll see you Saturday next, then. Yours, Peter T. Lockland.' "

Katie sighed. "Yours . . . ," she repeated, and floated into our bedroom. I was sure she'd be in there stuffing old rags in her brassiere. I reckoned this fool'd be like all the others. He'd break Katie's heart, and once again I'd have to be at the ready with some new jokes and Jack tales when it happened. Katie wasn't allowed to go on dates, but she'd had her fair share of heartbreak from the fellas who'd come sniffing around here.

"Jeez," I muttered, then slid my eyes at Mama to make sure she hadn't heard me. But she was far too busy gobbling up that sinful syrup. I pushed away from the table, stomped to the front porch, and flopped into one of the old rockers. Why did I have to stick around for Katie's stupid beau to turn up? It was Saturday! A gal should be able to grab a patch of shade and kick back on a Saturday.

Thankfully, Cody strolled up to the porch a few minutes later. Unthankfully, he toted a fishing pole and basket.

"Let's go to Abrams Creek," he said.

I shook my head. "Can't. Gotta wait for the fella Katie's been necking with."

I hadn't realized Gramps was on the porch, too. But he just snorted and dropped into the rocker next to mine. He leaned his Remington Parker against the table between us.

"You up for a little fun?" he muttered, and jutted his chin toward the swinging suspension bridge.

Crossing it was Peter T. himself—a good two hours earlier than we were expecting him.

Gramps sucked his teeth while old Peter lumbered across the dusty yard. I hadn't seen a twinkle in Gramps's eyes in weeks, so I was happy to see a spark there now. The young man stopped at the bottom step of the porch and pulled at his starched collar. I have to admit, he looked right dashing in his button-up shirt and hat.

"Mr. Tipton, sir, I'm here to accompany your lovely granddau—"

"Whew-ee, son!" Gramps threw back his head, opened up his nostrils, and sucked in a huge breath. "You stink worse'n two hogs in August. You walk here all the way from the Sugarlands, boy?"

Peter T. shook his head. "No, sir, I rode my—"

"Whoo, son. I gotta tell you, you're smellin' mighty stout. Whyn't you go warsh up in the springs over there?" Gramps raised a crooked finger and pointed to the far end of the yard.

"But sir, I—"

Gramps picked up the shotgun and opened the chamber, as if to check for shells. Cody sucked in a sharp breath like Gramps might really fire the thing, and Peter T. hightailed it over to that spring faster than a snap. I put my hand over my mouth to cover my grin. If this fella was anything like the others that had come sniffing around Katie in the last few years, there was no way he'd go through with it. But there stood Katie's new beau, splashing water all over his Sunday bests. Every once in a while he'd look over his shoulder at the porch.

"The armpits, too, boy!" Gramps yelled. He stood and made the motions of someone lathering his underarms. "Get 'em good and wet, now." I tried to make my shoulders stop shaking.

"Mr. Tipton, sir," Cody whispered, "don't be too hard on him." Gramps waved him off.

After about ten minutes of soaking, Gramps nodded at Peter T., who slopped back over to where we rocked. He was wet but darned determined.

"Sir, I—"

"Son, you think I'm gonna let you in my house like that?" Gramps waved his wrist at poor Peter T. "You're wetter than a sip of water. You sit right down on that rock over there"—he pointed at a huge boulder pushing out of the yard—"and dry out. Ain't no sponges comin' in my house today, sonny."

I spit a giggle. A little of the fight left Peter T.'s eyes, and he turned and squished toward the rock. He climbed atop it and wrung out his necktie.

A few minutes later, Cody shifted in his rocking chair. "Mr. Tipton? He looks drier now, doesn't he? Whyn't you let him off the hook?" Gramps either ignored him or didn't hear him.

After a good half hour or so of rock squatting, old Peter T. was starting to get a mite squirmy. Course, it's durn near impossible to get comfortable on a rock.

Gramps beckoned to the boy. "Son, you look to be less wet now. You ready for me to call out my girl?"

Peter T. sprang to his feet and raced to the foot of the stairs. "Yessir!" There was no denying that he was itching to see his Kathryn.

"Whoa there, hotfoot!" Gramps eked down the stairs and adjusted Peter T.'s shirt at the shoulders. "Don't you think you're a bit empty-handed?"

Peter T. looked at his hands dumbly. Gramps rolled his eyes. Cody rapped his feet on the porch—*tap-tap-tap-tap-tap*.

"Flowers, son!" Gramps said. "You think a romantic girl like Katie—er, *Kathryn*—don't want flowers from her beau?"

Peter T. looked like he might cry. Gramps wiped a wrinkled hand down his face, pulling the loose skin around his mouth taut. I couldn't tell if he'd have mercy on old Pete or not. I *could* tell Cody wanted him to. Real bad.

Gramps slung an arm around Peter T.'s shoulders. "They's a patch of trillium down by the bridge."

Peter T. nodded till it looked like his head would bob off. He dashed down to the bridge, hastily grabbed a handful of white flowers, and scurried back to the porch.

"Now hang on there, son," Gramps said, and picked a petal off one of the flowers. "These look a mite droopy to me. . . ."

"Sir!" Cody shouted, and sprang from his chair. His eyes were squinched closed behind his glasses, like he was afraid of seeing what would happen next. "Isn't anything ever good enough for you?"

It was so loud and so sudden, it felt like a shotgun had exploded and my ears were still ringing. I knew Cody meant this here situation, but those words served to underline what I reckon everyone in the Cove had been thinking secretly for weeks: Gramps had lost their everything.

Cody jiggled some rocks around in his pocket.

"My dad, he shucked some red corn once, too," he said. I gathered he meant his parents had met the same way Katie and Peter T. did. It was the closest he'd come to mentioning his mama since the telegram.

Peter T. finally broke the long silence. "Sir, I'm here to accompany your lovely granddaughter on an outing."

Gramps's face slowly pulled into a wide, yellow grin. "Now that's more like it, son," he said. His hand was on Peter T.'s shoulder, but he was looking at Cody. "I like a man that'll stick up for hisself."

13

I do things different. It helps to remind yourself of that when you usher your sister toward that fancy honeymoon suite at the Wonderland Motel in Gatlinburg.

Things started disappearing around the cabin, but I didn't say nothing. It wasn't much at first: a silver teapot here, an old shotgun there. Then bigger stuff: the old plow rusting next to the barn, a fat hog ready for slaughter but from which we never saw meat. I thought maybe Mama was swiping these goods to pay for groceries, until I stumbled upon what appeared to be a secretive meeting in the barn-turned-hotel between Gramps and some smallish outsider sporting a bowtie. Gramps had gone and hired some expensive Knoxville lawyer and was hocking his stuff to foot the bill! Here's what I overheard:

"Mr. Tipton, I have to say our chances of winning don't look very good."

"You think I don't know that, Mr. Polk? But I gotta do somethin'."

"I understand. That's why I decided to take your case. You and your neighbors haven't been treated fairly."

Gramps snorted. "Oh, we been treated fairly. Fairly rotten."

Every time I turned around, there were Peter T. and Katie—canoodling on the front porch, near the barn, next to the creek. Mama kept her eagle eyes on them, demanding that she be able to see the Holy Ghost between them at all times. But if Mama turned her head for one second, Katie would nuzzle up under Peter T.'s chin like a kitten. Peter T. beamed like the North Star.

So it was a surprise when one day after school,

while Gramps and I were gathering honey from the beehives, Peter T. approached us by himself. Gramps grinned at him and dusted his hands on his overalls.

"Why, Peter T.! I was beginning to think that you couldn't walk without my granddaughter hooked on your elbow."

Peter T. blushed and scratched his chin. "If I might have a word, sir?"

Gramps nodded and looked at me as if to dismiss me. I turned to set down the crate of Ball jars I was holding. They clinked like tiny church bells as I did.

"Autumn, you can stay," Peter T. said, and smiled. I think it was the first time he'd spoken to me directly. His eyes met mine, and I noticed they were a surprising shade of amber like the honey we'd collected. "I'd like your blessing, too."

I was more than a little taken aback that he wanted me to stay, but I didn't let on. Most of Katie's beaus don't even bat an eyelash at me. I set the crate down on a tree stump and folded my arms across my chest to hear him out.

Peter T. took a deep breath, and the words came spilling out of him like water through a sieve. "I really love your granddaughter—your sister, Autumn—and I know that most times a man is supposed to wait and ask permission from the father about these things, but he's gone so much and I just got this job offer in Maryville, see, so I'd be moving next month and I'd like nothing better than to take Kathryn along with me as my bride."

He was so winded at the end of this confession that I drew in a deep breath for him. Then I looked at Gramps. I expected some teeth sucking, followed by a string of embarrassing chores put upon old Peter T. But instead Gramps turned to me, head cocked.

"Autumn—you know more 'bout Katie's past beaus and whatnot to be able to tell: is Peter here a stand-up guy?"

My throat tightened up. *I* was gonna be the one to grant this fella permission to propose to my sister? No. I couldn't let Katie go. She'd been the only one on my side since this park mess began. We were in this together, she and I. Together we worried about Pop's job. Together we helped keep Mama from being so lonely. Together we were gonna move to Knoxville, make new friends. I didn't want to go it alone.

Peter's amber eyes fell on me, and I don't think I've ever had another human being look at me like that. The longing in those eyes was as dark and deep as Tuckaleechee Caverns. It was almost as if my answer would echo off him.

I do things different. It helps to remind yourself of that when you feel the power over the fate of others pulling at the tip of your tongue.

I reeled in my heartstrings and felt a grin spread across my face. "Yep. This one's a keeper, Gramps."

Two weeks later, I thought I might upchuck every time I caught a glimpse of myself. I looked like a dandelion. No, wait—too simple. A baby chick. No—not frilly enough. I looked like a baby chick in a tutu made of dandelions perched on a yellow-frosted cupcake setting on a yellow lace doily. Yep, that's it.

'Twas my sister-of-the-bride dress. Jeez!

I eyeballed myself in the mirror in our bedroom one last time—I'd probably looked at my reflection more today than I had in the rest of my life combined. It'd take every last bit of gumption I could muster to parade down the aisle of the Missionary Baptist Church in this getup. But it was for Katie. I could do it.

"Autumn! How's my favorite season?" I whirled

around to see Pop filling the doorway. He threw back his blond head and laughed his big, hearty chuckle.

I leapt toward him and gave him the biggest hug my arms could give. "Looking more like summer, I'd say." I scowled down at the yellow poof.

Pop tweaked the huge bow resting atop my head. "Summer's nice too, you know."

I hadn't seen him since the night of the school-house meeting, when he'd had to hightail it back to his job site before his supervisor noticed he was gone. I was so full of questions I thought I might bust. "Pop, what're we gonna do when—"

"Father," Katie said. Pop and I turned and watched her drift into the room like a warm breeze. Her long blue organdy dress kissed the floor, just hiding her feet. The ring of daisies in her hair made her look downright angelic. It looked like she was floating. I think she was. Funny thing, too, 'cause Katie's never been known for her grace. She's tall and big-boned, as Mama likes to say, but today she looked airy and fragile.

Pop's green eyes glistened. "Katie," he sighed, and gave her a huge hug. "You look like a dream."

"Thanks, Daddy," she whispered. They hugged for a full minute before Pop straightened.

"Mighty quick courtship, you and Paul," he said.

"Peter." Katie rolled her eyes. She licked her thumb and swiped at my already-scrubbed-clean cheek. It took everything I had not to tackle her and give her an Indian burn.

"So why the rush, Katie-pie?" Pop asked.

"Daddy," Katie said, "you know full well that Peter's job in Maryville starts next week."

"Hey, speaking of jobs—" I started.

Mama rushed through the door, all spinning and sputtering and dizzy. "Katie, Autumn, Gus—get your tails in the wagon this minute!" Boy, she must've been flustered, to use the word "tail"! "We've got to get to the church and set up the games before it gets hotter than Hades!" Wow—"Hades," too! This was going to be some day.

I linked my arm in Pop's and led him toward the door. "Sit by me, Pop. I gotta ask you about—"

Pop gave my hand a quick squeeze. "Later, bug," he whispered. "Today is Katie's big day." He hoisted himself into the back of the wagon. Mama, Katie, and Gramps rode on the bench up front. We weren't but a mile or so down the road when the horse right in front of Katie shifted his hindquarters and relieved himself.

"Eeeeewww!" Katie shrieked. She stood and fanned herself with her fingertips. "I'm gonna stink!"

Mama glared at Gramps. "What on earth are you feeding these horses, Daddy?" Gramps grunted and shrugged.

Pop tilted his head back and inhaled a big whiff, like horse manure was the freshest-smelling thing since French perfume. "Boy, will I ever miss this place," he whispered.

It made me sad knowing that Pop would never live here again. He'd only moved to Knoxville a few months back. Before that, he'd lived in the Cove his whole life. Born in the house right next to the one where Mama was born. Now both those houses had been torn down.

I leaned toward Pop so no one on the bench could hear me. "I'm sorry we didn't get the chance to sell our art, Pop. That sure would've been a nice job."

The tip of Pop's nose turned bright red, just like mine does right before the tears well up. But he clenched his jaw, straightened his shoulders, and smiled down at me. "They's always more jobs, Autumn. They's but one Cades Cove."

Katie and Peter T. jumped the broom, and Pop had to skeedaddle to get back to work before his supervisor docked his pay. He didn't say another word about the park or his job or nothing, but don't think I didn't try. I got the impression he didn't answer my questions because he *couldn't* answer my questions. And don't think that made me feel at ease.

It was a fine November day, all blue sky and puffy clouds dotting the mountaintops. The biddies bustled around, each one making a bigger fuss over Katie than the last, and Katie soaked it all up like a dishrag. Uncle John and Uncle John Too and the boys broke out their fiddles, and Mama didn't even stop them. She was too busy placing the last few sprigs of wildflowers atop the wedding cake. Yum! My sweet tooth had been pining for that cake ever since Peter T. dropped to one knee.

All the folks who came to the wedding—everyone in the Cove, plus a few of Peter T.'s kin from the Sugarlands—played Whoopee Hide in the cemetery behind the church after the wedding. I just watched. Boy, was I ever glum.

Tilly McBroom snuck over to me and flipped open a tin can, one that used to house bandages. Inside were tiny plugs of chewing tobacco. I cut my eyes around the churchyard before sneaking a pouch between my bottom lip and gums. The tobacco tasted icky-sweet and naughty—kinda like our whiskey syrup.

"Don't let your mama see I give you that," Tilly said, and spit onto the grass. Suddenly I wasn't sure where I should spit, this being the church grounds and my sister's wedding and all, so I just swallowed.

Things were quiet a moment before she added, "Tell your gramps I said thank you."

At first I thought she was being sassy about the park, so I turned on my heel toward her. "What?"

"I knowed it was him that left that wad of money on my doorstep. He'd never admit it, though. He thinks he owes us something 'cause he talked us into supporting that park. He don't owe us squat. But that money sure come in handy about now."

A trickle of tobacco juice slid down my throat. Part of the money Gramps was getting from hocking all his stuff was going to our neighbors? I knew an awful lot of his stuff had gone missing, but I thought all of it was going to that fancy-pants lawyer.

"Autumn, honey, run in the church and grab that basket of eggs and a fistful of spoons." Mama appeared, shaking me out of my doldrums. " 'Bout time for the egg races to get under way."

I nodded and ducked inside the cool church, scooping out the plug of tobacco and flinging it into the dirt before I did. It took a few seconds for my eyes to regulate from the bright sunlight outside. The church smelled like both dust and dust polish, if that's possible. It was empty, save for the limp decorations and strands of wildflowers we'd strung up this morning. I plunked down in a pew, covered my eyes, and sprawled out. Heaven help me for putting my feet up on a pew, but I felt like God might understand.

My stomach clenched up as I took yet another tally of all the things I'd lost or would lose in the next few weeks:

↔ My pop's job
↔ My old house
↔ Gramps's farm
↔ My neighbors (though their trust seemed to be intact, which was more than I'd given them credit for)
↔ My new house in Knoxville
↔ And now my sister, who I'd always thought I'd love to see married off, but as it turned out . . . I didn't. She was the only one who was always on my side with this park. I didn't know who was

on my side anymore. Truth be told, I didn't even know what my side *was*. But Katie always seems to know where she stands.

And then, as if she'd heard me being nice to her in my head, Katie said, "Autumn Winifred Oliver! You get your feet off that pew this instant."

I opened my eyes to see her hovering over me like a crow over a dead possum. I sat up, and when I did, tears slid down my cheeks. I hadn't even known I'd been crying, it'd been so long since I'd done it.

Katie pushed me gently on the shoulder. "Scootch." I scooted down the pew and she dropped in next to me, her wedding dress draping over my poofy skirt. She started tugging on her earlobe the instant she sat down.

"You can come see me in Maryville."

"It's a two-day trip."

She shrugged, but it was more of a *yeah . . .* shrug than a *so?* shrug. "I'll write you every day."

I snorted out a laugh before I could stop myself. Katie writing letters! I smiled. "You gonna balance the ledgers, too?"

A grin snuck across her face. "Okay, so I won't write you every day. But, um . . ." She reached over me and grabbed an egg out of the basket next to me. "Got some ink?"

I wasn't sure what she was up to, but I found some ink and an old-timey quill in the table behind the altar. Katie dipped the quill and wrote on the egg:

Autumn Winifred Oliver
Cades Cove, Tenn.
Write me!

"Katie—"

"Shush, now." Katie grabbed my elbow and pulled me out the door into the searing sunlight. She scanned the yard, then yanked me toward Jeremiah Butler. He looked like he'd been tipping back some happy juice, based on the smile he was sporting. (Or syrup, perhaps.)

"The blushing bride!" Jeremiah slurred, then hiccupped. "And her hooligan sister." He tried to whisper that last part, but it came out just as loud. My stomach flopped over. I didn't feel so hot.

"Jeremiah," Katie said, grabbing one of his shoulders, "sell this egg at market tomorrow, will you?" She put the egg in his hand.

"I can't sell this." He held the egg up to the

sunlight and tried to read Katie's handwriting. "It's all . . . gaumy."

Katie rolled her eyes at me, then turned and batted her eyelashes at Jeremiah. I knew she was up to something 'cause her earlobe was getting worked over nice. "Oh, you. Just slip it in with the rest of your stock. No one will even notice. Consider it my wedding present." She tilted her head and flipped her bouncy hair.

Jeremiah turned about six shades of red. "Will do, Katie. And happy, uh . . . wedding."

Katie pulled me aside. "There," she whispered, giving me a peck on the cheek before flitting away toward the wedding cake. "You may not get a letter from *me* that often, but you'll hear from somebody!"

Katie and Peter T. divvied up the cake and started handing out huge hunks of it. Cake—*ugh*. I tasted all that tobacco juice I'd swallowed rise up in the back of my throat. I ran over to the bushes and heaved so hard, I thought I might see my toes come flying out.

Add to that list of things I'd lost:

↔ My lunch

14

I do things different.
It helps to remind
yourself of that
when you're
duping tourists
for cash money.

Three days later, I trudged home from school and went straight to the room I now shared with just Mama. I lay sprawled across my bed, hand tucked under my mattress, fingertips barely touching the stick of dynamite that still lay in wait. I must've looked like a hyena that'd lost its laugh, because Mama came into our little nook of a bedroom, took one look at me, and said, "Winnie, you got to stop breathing water."

Mama uses all these sayings, but this one was new to me. "Come again?"

"Your granny used to say that." Mama smiled like she could hear *her* mama's voice just then. She wrapped a quilt around my shoulders. "You don't even notice the air you breathe. Until you have to breathe water."

I nodded, and we sat there all quiet for another bit. It was nice.

"You'd be breathing water in Knoxville, wouldn't you, Mama?"

Mama nodded. "I'm afraid I'd breathe water anywhere but the Cove, Winnie."

I saw something then in Mama's eyes I hadn't noticed before: a small black spot, a tiny pool of sadness and worry. "You wanted this park, too, didn't you? You and Pop and Gramps all wanted this."

Mama blinked several times, but the pool didn't wash away. I knew I was right.

"Gramps is breathing water, too."

Mama thought about that one for a moment. "Has been since your granny died."

Over Mama's shoulder and out the front door, the leather britches beans we'd strung together at the Syrup Soppin' Festival began to rustle. We'd carted them home from the festival and tacked them to the eaves of the front porch to dry. Now the wind scratched through them, and the dry strings of beans eked out a parched tune. The dust that'd gathered on them over the past few weeks blew off and danced in sparkly sunlit circles before disappearing.

I finally 'fessed up. "Mama, I'm scared."

I expected Mama to tell me that the Lord will provide, to trust her and Pop, to stop acting like such a baby. But instead, Mama hugged me close. "I'm scared, too, Winnie."

Now, how it is that I felt *better* knowing that, I don't know. I hugged her back. "Well, then, we'll just be scared together."

The next day after school, Gramps dragged Cody and me halfway up Gregory Bald in search of chestnuts. The afternoon was cold and our feet crunched through piles of crackly brown leaves.

We'd walked for nearly two miles and had seen nary a chestnut.

"In my day," Gramps grumbled, "chestnuts covered the ground this time of year. Why, they was so many of them . . ."

I sighed. The old-timers were fond of telling us

young'uns how many chestnuts there *used* to be. Blight swept through and killed most of the trees a decade or so back. You'd think chestnuts were chiseled from solid gold, the way they went on and on about them.

Gramps paused, then commenced to suck his teeth. "They was so many chestnuts, you could get a running head start, jump atop the lot of them, and roll all the way to Gatlinburg."

I pictured Gramps as a boy (broader shoulders but same shriveled head) skating on a pile of chestnuts, bony elbows and knocky knees flying everywhere. The thought of it made me titter. Cody must've been thinking the same thing, because he laughed, too. I almost didn't hear the snap of a twig behind us.

"C'mere!" Gramps whispered. He grabbed my elbow in one hand, Cody's in the other, and pulled us behind a huge birch. He pointed downhill at the broad, new hiking trail carving its way up the side of the mountain. "Tourists!"

I peeked around the broad tree at the couple hefting themselves toward us. The man sported a bright orange vest with a thousand pockets, and a pair of binoculars swung from his neck. The woman

wore a floppy straw hat and fanned herself with a
store-bought map, though her breath showed in the
cool air in tiny puffs.

"My goodness, Philip," she sniffed. Her voice
came out of her nose instead of her mouth, seemed
like. "Did we have to start on the trail marked 'ad-
vanced'?"

Gramps bent in half and pulled off his boots.
"Quick—take off your shoes!"

Cody shot me a look full of question marks, but I
shrugged and kicked off my Mary Janes. Cody followed suit.

Gramps tucked in a plug of tobacco, sucked his
teeth, and ran his eyes over Cody and me.

"Don't say nothing. *Nothing.*" He popped out
from behind the birch onto the trail and nearly
scared the pants off the couple.

"Howdy," he mumbled, then spit right near their
feet. The husband took a step backwards and almost
fell over a tree root.

"Oh, Philip, look!" the woman cried. "Moun-
taineers!" She caught sight of me and Cody, leaned
over, and pinched my cheek so hard I thought I might
have to pinch her right back. "Aren't they cute?

"Where are your shoes, sweetie-pie?" she yelled

at me, like I didn't understand English or something. I looked at Gramps.

He shook his head. "She don't talk, ma'am. Not since the accident."

Talks Through Her Nose sucked in a quick breath. "Accident? Oh, my!" She turned to Cody. "Your shoes?" she shouted at him, and pointed at his feet.

Cody played along and danced a quick jig. Pretty funny, if you ask me.

Gramps sighed real showy-like. "Well, he surely can't talk neither, ma'am. He's only nine."

Talks Through Her Nose gasped. She wheeled around and snapped her fingers at her husband. "Philip, give them some money. These poor children need shoes." She waved her open hand in front of Philip until he laid three one-dollar bills in it. Three dollars!

Gramps shook his head. "Oh, no thanky, ma'am. We surely can't take no charity." He was laying on his words extra thick. I could hardly understand him myself.

"What?" Talks Through Her Nose yelled at him. "Oh, no *charity*! Yes, yes, I see. . . ." She tapped the side of her thick head like it took some jarring to move those dusty old thoughts around inside.

"Ah, yes!" she shouted again at Gramps. "Can I *pay* you to take a picture with me? One dollar each? With a camera?" She made the motion of clicking a photo with her hands.

Gramps shook his head. "Camera . . . ?" Oh, boy. She had to feel her leg getting pulled now.

But old Talks Through Her Nose snapped again at her hubby, who pulled a boxy Kodak from one of his many pockets. "A *camera* . . ." She showed Gramps the contraption. He shrugged.

"He doesn't understand you, Claire," Philip chimed in, like Gramps wasn't standing right there.

But Talks Through Her Nose—Claire—was pushing us and shoving us and arranging us next to a mountain laurel bush. "You stand there, and you get right there . . . perfect!" She wriggled between me and Cody and pulled Gramps over behind me. "Say cheese—I mean, uh, *smile*!"

Philip clicked the shutter and the flashbulb went off with a lightning-bolt pop.

"Arrrgghhhh!" Gramps growled, and jammed his fists in his eyes. "I'm blinded! You done blinded me with your devil box! Git! Git now! Git thee behind me, Satan!"

Talks Through Her Nose and Philip hopped back down that mountain like two fleas trying to outrun a vinegar wash on a mangy mutt. The three of us bowled over laughing, me so hard I thought I might pee. Through my teary eyes, I saw the crisp dollar bills laying on the pine straw.

Gramps balled up the money and stuffed it in the front pocket of his overalls. "Might be the only money we ever see from this park."

15

I do things different.
It helps to remind
yourself of that
when you haunt
the Missionary
Baptist church.

I began to think Gramps was deliberately trying to cheer me up, because the very next day he came in and grabbed me by my elbow, hefting me off my spot on the floor in front of the fire.

"C'mon, girl, we got errands to run."

Errands? Gramps doesn't run errands—things come to *him*.

We loaded into the cart. I bundled under a wool blanket that carried the musty smell of horse. It was a cool day, but the sun shone down in yellow ribbons from a sky so big and so blue it made your eyes ache for something less dazzling. But finding that wasn't as easy as it sounds. The trees had turned into a showy blaze of orange and red and yellow bursts—miniature suns, each one. Those durn trees! They put on this spectacle every year, and I swannee they get better at it with practice.

Somebody on a nearby farm was burning leaves. There's something about the dusty-dry smell of smoke rising off a pile of charred leaves that makes me think too much. So I usually don't cotton to the scent, but today it seemed like the afternoon's perfume.

Gramps pointed a crooked, shaky finger at the puff of smoke. "It's too big. Somebody doesn't know what they's doing, burning all them leaves at once."

We clip-clopped toward the now-black cloud of smoke and soon realized it was coming from the general area of the Missionary Baptist Church.

"Dadburned CCC boys!" Gramps whipped the team of horses to speed them up. "Hee-yah!"

When we got to the church, there was nary a soul in sight. The pile of leaves was burning near the cemetery. The danger wasn't that the fire was too close to the church; the danger was that the fire was too tall. Way too tall. If it kept burning like it was, it'd stretch right up and start licking the dry leaves on the trees overhead. If those caught fire, there was no telling how far and how fast the flames could go. Maybe through the whole Cove.

I ran to grab a bucket from the storage closet inside the church, then dashed to the pump and put my whole weight behind the up-and-down motion it took to draw off a pail of water. I hefted the full bucket back to the fire and dumped it at the edge of the leaf pile. A handful of leaves sizzled for a moment, then the fire crawled right around the small wet spot. This fire was hungry. And hot.

Gramps had found a rake and was reaching into the flames, thinning out the pile of leaves so the fire couldn't climb as high. It was working, but not fast enough. He threw the rake at me and yelled, "Spread 'em as thin as you can! Don't get burnt!"

And then I saw something I'll never forget if I live to be a hundred and two. Gramps began stomping the blaze like a crazed clogger. What a sight— Gramps dancing through flames like the devil hisself against the stark white outline of the Missionary Baptist Church. Heaven and hell, right here in Cades Cove!

I threw the head of the rake into the blaze, then

pulled it back toward me, flattening the fiery pile of leaves. I was careful not to let the handle catch fire. It couldn't've been hotter if I was standing on the face of the sun. The flames lapped at my elbows, and every once in a while, I had to leap backwards to keep from getting a fiery kiss on the cheek.

After a bunch of sweating and (Heaven help us for doing it on the church grounds) cussing, we finally got the leaves spread out thin enough. The fire dwindled to a few spitting flames. It was only at that point that we heard the *hardy-har-har* of a group of boys around the side of the church.

Gramps and I looked around the corner, him wheezing and sweating to beat all. Huddled there was a group of boys, including that uniformed nose honker hisself, Jonathon Parker.

He had his penknife out and was carving something. We stumbled closer.

Jonathon loves Mary 4-ever

Scratched into the side of *our church!* Jonathon thumped a fellow CCCer on the back and offered up his knife.

"Carve it up now, boys. This place is going to be seen by millions!"

If Gramps was even a hair as mad as I was, he didn't show it. Instead, he stepped forward, sucking his teeth.

"You boys sleeping in the church tonight?" he asked, patting the side of the building like a loyal old dog.

Jonathon and the rest of the CCC crew startled at his voice, but Jonathon straightened quickly. "Yep. Me and the boys"—at this, he twitched his thumb at the others—"we've got lots more work to do in this area before the park opens. Need to make it *presentable*, you know?"

Gramps clicked his tongue and shook his head. "Mighty sorry to hear it, boys. Last fella to spend a full night in here was Otis Plunk. Old Otis went loopy and hanged hisself from the rafters." Gramps jerked a pretend noose around his neck and made a gagging sound in the back of his throat.

"That was back in . . . aught five, I reckon. Still haunted, she is," he said, patting the wall again.

The CCC boys shifted a little in their khaki pants.

"Mean old haint, too. Otis's ghost, he tries to slip a noose around ever' neck that bares itself after midnight in this church. Killed three, maybe four others."

Then Gramps clapped. "Well, sleep tight, boys!" He spun on his boot heel and marched away.

I followed, and heard Jonathon behind me say, "Don't listen to that old-timer. He's all wet!"

I felt as unsettled as a pot of boiling water. "Gramps!" I yelled, and ran to catch up with him. "I got a real beef with that fella. Care to help me get his goat?"

A wide yellow grin stretched across Gramps's craggy face. "What you got in mind, girl?"

We returned to the church near midnight, with Cody in tow. Those hooligans must've talked themselves out of being fearful of any haints, because the church was dark as coal, and the lot of them was snoring to beat all.

Without so much as a peep, I led Jeb, our mangy old bloodhound, off the back of the wagon. He blinked at me with soft, trusting eyes. I scratched his graying nose. Drool dripped off his long jowls.

I do things different. It helps to remind yourself of that when you're about to turn loose an overweight, flatulent mutt in the Lord's house.

"Don't step on nobody, okay, Jeb?"

Cody and I shoved his rear end up the five steps leading to the church, and good old Jeb plodded directly inside. We scurried behind the maple out front where Gramps was already hiding. Us three could hear Jeb's toenails scratch across the pine plank floor in the church, then a bunch of rustling and snorting and huffing.

"Sweet Mary, Mother of Jesus!"

"It's Otis Plunk!"

"Spare us, Mr. Plunk! Spare our souls!"

That did it. Old Jeb started baying like he knew this was his one shot to sing in church. And whenever that dog bays, he farts. We could hear him passing that awful gas of his all the way outside. And then we could smell it—boy oh boy, could we smell it! Before anybody could light a lantern to see that this angel of death was just an ancient bloodhound, that church door flew open and a parade of pajamas streaked across the lawn.

A scrawny pair of red long johns appeared in the doorway, supported by the two bony shoulders of

Jonathon Parker. At first, I was disappointed because he wasn't crying, wasn't cussing, wasn't even blanched.

But when Gramps set eyes on him, he doubled over and laughed so hard he started to wheeze.

Cody pointed at the dark red spot running down the inside of Jonathon's leg, growing bigger and darker by the second.

I couldn't help myself. I cupped my hands around my mouth and yelled, "Hey, Jonathon—who's all wet?"

16

i do things different.
it helps to remind
yourself of that
when you play host
to the president of
these United States.

The next time I saw Gramps's lawyer—the bow-tie-wearing Mr. Polk—was the end of November. He and Gramps ducked into the barn, so I followed. I hovered in the hayloft, so I could hear everything down below. (I just prayed I wouldn't sneeze.) They whispered all hush-hush, but I overheard just enough.

"It's no use, Mr. Tipton. I can't file a single injunction without Chapman's team of lawyers from Nashville stomping it flat with an opposing injunction. If we don't drop our lawsuits, they're going to sue you and your neighbors right back."

"Sue us? What the devil for?"

"They're claiming eminent domain, which means—"

"I know what it means."

"—which means the federal government can buy any piece of land it needs for a fair price."

"They 'need' our land, eh?"

Mr. Polk cleared his throat. "For the park to be a success, yes. It's the most beautiful land I've ever seen, Mr. Tipton."

Gramps was silent. A first, I believe.

Mr. Polk continued. "As you know, park officials are offering to allow you and your neighbors the opportunity to lease the land back from the government and stay in the Cove. That's certainly a first. I doubt they would've offered that if you hadn't hired me." I felt myself growing hotter and hotter at this snotty Mr. Polk.

Gramps snorted. "Pay rent to farm our own land? A dollar an acre. Mighty steep."

"Well . . . yes. But I suggest we cease further legal action or they might withdraw that offer, too."

What? Mr. Polk was giving up on us after we'd

paid him all that money? But instead of hammering his fist into the guy's gut like I expected Gramps to do, he grabbed the lawyer's hand and pumped it in a huge handshake.

"Thanks again for taking our case, Mr. Polk. You sure I can't pay you nothing?"

"Not a penny, Mr. Tipton. This is the most meaningful pro bono case I've ever accepted."

Mr. Polk had worked for free? I did some quick figuring. All the money Gramps had made from pawning his stuff must've found its way to our other neighbors' doorsteps.

"I am sorry, Mr. Tipton," Mr. Polk said. "I wish I could do more."

"Me too, Mr. Polk. Me too."

Anybody with the middle name Delano is bound to be a little stuffy, if you ask me. But I can honestly report that in all of my eleven years, I'd never laid eyes upon a president. So when the big cheese himself— Franklin Delano Roosevelt—came to the area for the park's groundbreaking ceremony, I was one of the thousands of folks milling around for hours, pretending the early December rain and looming gray clouds were nothing but sunshine and blue skies.

What a spectacle! There were people cheering and flashbulbs popping and big, bendy radio microphones hoisted everywhere. (I was itching to yell "Autumn Winifred Oliver for president!" into one of them, but Cody talked me out of it.) There were even moving-picture cameras ticking off spool after spool of film. Mama said this newsreel might even be seen in California!

FDR was a tall man with spectacles and a mane of gray hair. The way he talks, you've got no choice but to listen—his voice booms and lilts and swings in all the right places. I'd heard him before on the radio during his fireside chats, but *seeing* him speak was like watching fire itself, all spark and crackle and fizz.

I really hadn't heard a word, though, until Mr. Roosevelt said that the Great Smoky Mountains rivaled the most beautiful places he'd ever seen. That struck me as funny—beauty having a rival. Seems like beauty would have nothing but friends. Nobody else seemed to think it was all that queer, though, so I went back to figuring out how I could get my mug into one of those newsreels.

I shouldn't have worried about that, because as

soon as Mr. Roosevelt's speech was done, some official-looking fella with a handlebar mustache and a heckuva grip grabbed me and Cody by the shirt collars.

"Line up, kids. Shoulder to shoulder. Smile nice, now. That's it."

It was nothing short of biblical. The sea of people parted, making a wide aisle in the middle of the crowd, and me and Cody somehow ended up on the front line. Within spitting distance of the president!

But then—oh, boy! Franklin Delano Roosevelt himself descended into the crowd. He walked with a limp and a cane, but you hardly noticed what with all the pumping of hands and nodding and smiling. Closer, closer, closer he came. . . .

"Beautiful home you have here, little lady." And then Franklin Delano Roosevelt ruffled my hair. My hair! Now there were two people alive allowed to do that.

Mama, three rows back, nearly fainted. "That's my girl!" she said to everyone around her who would listen. "She's destined for great things, that one."

I do things different. It helps to remind yourself of that when the most powerful man in the world just gave you a new hairdo.

17

I do things different.
It helps to remind
yourself of that
when you hear those
church bells tolling
once again.

Months. It'd been months since I'd hiked up to the Meadow in the Sky on old Thunderhead Mountain. We were on winter break from school, so I buckled my old leather book belt around my sketch pad and pencil case and scaled Thunderhead—the old way, not using those new trails. Tomorrow was Christmas, and I needed to finish up my drawings. I wouldn't be the only one *not* giving gifts again this year, no sir.

It was cold up there in the meadow, all right. When the wind got to whipping, it whistled right up through the naked trees and across the bleak meadow. The grass had bleached out and shriveled up, and the chill rustled the stalks in a way that was both sorry and peaceful.

Only the pine trees—stubborn old coots—still clung to their needles. What was it about those trees that made them think those prickly little wisps were worth holding on to all year long? Why, if pine trees were people, they'd be . . .

Yep! That was what I'd sketch for Gramps—a grove of pine trees! I smiled at my joke, then flipped open the drawing pad and began scratching out the rough, triangular outlines of the pines.

I'd just started adding the lowlights when I heard a tiny *achoo* behind me. I jumped higher than a long-tailed cat in a roomful of rocking chairs and whipped around to find myself staring at ten, maybe eleven boys and one man—all decked out in the same drab clothing.

Boy Scouts. I knew it would come to this.

"Oh, 'scuse us, little lady," the scoutmaster said. He smiled, and I could see by the crinkles near his eyes that he smiled a lot. "Didn't mean to scare you. Just passing through. March on, boys!"

The troop shifted into a near-perfect line and began to traipse off down the newly hatcheted trail. One of the boys stopped short.

"Mr. Morris, sir?" the boy drawled, and I could tell he was from around these parts. Not the Cove, but nearby. "Do you hear a bell?"

I leapt off the rustling grass and cocked my ear downwind so I could hear better. Yep, there it was—the church bell.

It rang right past eleven and kept on tolling—*ding, dong, ding*—to fifty-one. Whew—no one in my family. (Heaven help me for saying it!)

"Fifty-one," I must've muttered.

The scout shook his head. "Fifty-three."

Fifty-three? That was how many winters Gramps had under his belt.

"No!" I scrambled down the trail, clutching my sketch to my chest.

No. No—somewhere down there, five thousand feet below, Gramps was hiding, listening to that bell tote up his number, sucking his teeth, laughing at his cleverness. "Another prank, it is," I whispered.

Doc Tillman's best guess is Gramps died of a heart attack. I think he meant a broken heart.

My senses disappeared—there was nothing to see

but gray sky and black mountains, nothing to hear but the silence of snowflakes, nothing to smell but wet dirt. I felt blah and numb, like the wintry, sleeping trees that lumbered all around, dry and scratchy and reaching for naught.

And so even though the bells didn't toll for me that day, I still felt like I'd died.

I always thought that God somehow knew when funerals were happening, because in my memory, I recall every one I'd been to previously as being cold and dark and rainy. But Gramps must've sweet-talked God into teasing us, because his funeral was on a sunny and warm late December day. It was warm enough for the frost to disappear, for the pine trees to give off the sweet smell of sap, for Mama to worry about the mayonnaise in the potato salad turning sour. But the earth was cold. We were told it had taken hours for the pallbearers to hack through the frozen ground.

The Right Reverend Feezell was just about to lower the lid on the coffin when I got my gumption up.

"Wait!" I yelled. I ran to the open casket and placed my sketch of those ornery old pine trees in the box next to Gramps's still chest. It was my best drawing yet.

"It's a piece of the Cove," I whispered, then added even softer, "and a joke, too. You, pine trees . . . get it?"

Up till now, it had been my plan to bury the stick of dynamite I'd had stashed under my mattress these past few months with Gramps, too. But suddenly that didn't seem right. I touched my dress and felt the place where I'd tucked the explosive beneath my knickers. No. No dynamite in the Cove. I stepped back. Katie smiled at me, rubbing her earlobe, and I knew I'd made the right choice. Boy, was I happy to see her.

The good reverend closed the casket and the pallbearers lowered it into the ground with long, sturdy ropes. Mama rubbed my back and Peter T. rubbed Katie's back. Then we watched Pop and Uncle John and Uncle John Too and about twenty other relatives shovel piles of dirt into the deep hole. The first few shovelfuls landed with a hollow thud on the coffin below, but the hole slowly filled and the dirt made a tidy pile above the ground. Then the pallbearers laid their shovels in a big X across the dirt to show an end to work and toil.

When Pop placed Gramps's headstone, Cody came

over and held my hand and I didn't even stop him. Thousands of people would be gawking at this headstone every year, and not a one of them would be Gramps's kin. I knew Gramps would've already thought of that when he told Mama—on his deathbed, no doubt—what he wanted it to read. I read the marble slab:

Thomas Reginald Tipton
And the eyes of them both were opened.
—Genesis 3:7

Adam and Eve. But boy, "them" sure did feel like me and Gramps. Gramps had taken a bite of the apple, all right, but he didn't gain any knowledge of good and evil. Sometimes it's too hard to tell. What's good and what's evil, that is.

And then I laughed. Inappropriate, yes. Cody lifted his eyebrows at me and jerked his head at the pile of dirt as if to say, *We're at a* funeral, *Autumn*.

I whispered out of the corner of my mouth, "At least the headstone doesn't say, 'What the hell are you lookin' at?'"

18

I do things different.
It helps to remind
yourself of that
when you realize
that having the
knowledge of good
and evil and knowing
the good from the evil
are two different things.

Five standstill days after Gramps's death, a crisp,
white letter was delivered by Jeremiah Butler. Our
address was typed in crooked, jumpy letters on the
envelope.

Mama ripped it open. Her eyes filled with tears as
she read. Her hands shook, and the only sound in
the cabin was the crinkling of paper. She dropped
the letter and it floated to the floor.

December 27, 1934

Dear Mrs. Martha Oliver,

It has come to our attention that the lessee of plot 7 in Cades Cove, Tennessee—one Mr. Thomas Reginald Tipton—is recently deceased. As he was legally listed as the sole lessee of plot 7, the ownership of said property hereby reverts to the United States government upon his death. Please consider this letter your notice of eviction. We request that you permanently evacuate the premises by January 1, 1935.

The United States Park Service

P.S. Our deepest sympathies for your loss.

One week! One lousy week to pack up our lives and get out. Somebody really hightailed it to get us this letter this fast.

But oh, it was a banner day for us, mail-wise. Jeremiah delivered a second letter, this one worn, yellowed, and musty, like it'd been found at the bottom of a forgotten mailbag.

November 25, 1934

Dear Autumn Winifred Oliver of Cades Cove, Tennessee,

My name is Mary Elizabeth McGovern (but everyone calls me Puss because they say I look like a cat), and I live in New York City, New York. I am fourteen. My mother bought an egg from a pushcart on Orchard Street with your name on it, so I thought I'd write to you. Hello from New York!

My mother read that your city is being adopted into the new Great Smoky Mountains National Park. What an honor to have your home turned into a national park! If they did that in my neighborhood, all's they'd get is a few fish markets and some newspaper stands. My mother also says that she read there's just one road in and out of Cades Cove. One road! How exciting to have a pen pal in such an exotic location. Please write me back and tell me all about Cades Cove. My mother says we might make the drive to Tennessee to visit the Great Smoky Mountains on our next vacation. We could meet and you could be our official tour guide. I bet you do that a lot, though.

My best to you and yours,
Mary Elizabeth McGovern, aka. Puss
P.S. I have red hair. Do you? I ask because your name is Autumn. That's a pretty name. Much prettier than Puss. Being a redhead is hard because it's so different, isn't it?

But for all our mail that day, there was still no letter from Mr. John D. Rockefeller.

On my last day in the Cove, I went to say goodbye to Gramps. I blamed the tears in my eyes on the sunlight glinting off his silvery sleek headstone. The dirt over his grave was still muddy fresh. My leg itched, as I had the stick of dynamite tucked into my knickers. The rest of my life had been packed away in boxes and crates, all except for this stick of dynamite. I wasn't sure what to do with it. I thought Mama might question a cardboard box labeled "Explosives."

It was so quiet at the cemetery, and I enjoyed the peace. Then the roar of an automobile cut through the silence. I didn't turn when Cody appeared beside me.

"Your mama said you'd be here."

I nodded, and glanced over his shoulder at the shiny black Ford parked below. We stood there looking at Gramps's headstone as if we expected it to give us further instructions. A minute or so passed without us saying nothing.

Then the sunlight disappeared. To my left, a tall man in a black trench coat had stepped in front of the sun's rays, blocking the light, casting a long shadow over Cody and me.

"Miss Oliver," Colonel Chapman said. I don't think anyone had ever called me that before. "My sympathies for your loss."

I felt like my tongue had been stung by a swarm of bees, it was so obvious I didn't know what to say. Colonel Chapman shifted, and a patch of sunlight sprang around him and blinded me.

"Your granddaddy was . . ." Colonel Chapman paused and closed his eyes, as if he was reading this speech off the inside of his eyelids. "He was the toughest man I ever met."

With that, he turned on his heel and flounced toward his Ford, parked at the bottom of the hill.

Cody leaned over my shoulder. "Sorry 'bout that. He offered to give me a ride to say goodbye."

I shrugged with one shoulder. " 'S okay." Then I guess it was the setting or something, but I finally gathered up my gumption and said what I should've said long ago. "Sorry 'bout your mama, Cody."

Cody tried to mirror me: he shrugged one shoulder, too. But his eyes glassed over with tears, magnified by those awful glasses of his. " 'S okay."

We stood in silence for another minute before Cody said, "You leaving tomorrow, then?"

I nodded. "You staying put?"

He swiped at the corner of his eye with the back of his hand, but he grinned. He pulled something out of his coat pocket and thrust it at me. Three of the best rocks from his collection: a wavy, palm-sized phyllite, a sugar-sparkly quartzite, and some chunky slate. "It's a going-away present."

"Rocks?" I asked.

The corners of Cody's mouth turned up. "So you can put hexes on all those mean city folks."

I shook my head. "No, so I can chuck them on their rooftops when they need to repent."

Cody and me laughed. But I shook my head. "I can't take those, Cody," I said. "They're the best part of your collection."

Cody looked at the trio of rocks in his hand and

seemed to be considering the consequences of *not* giving them to me, now that he'd offered. Then a light came on behind his eyes. "I know!"

The tip of his tongue peeked out of his mouth as he dug in his pants pocket. He withdrew his hand, opened his fist, and there sat the shiniest penny I'd ever seen.

"My lucky penny. Take it."

I smirked. "You don't have a lucky penny."

"I do now." Cody placed the coin in my hand. He smiled at me, gave me a quick hug before I could stop him, then turned and slid down the rocky slope toward his uncle's car. " 'Bye, *Winnie*," he said over his shoulder. He'd been waiting for months to call me that, I bet. Only did it when he was out of reach, too.

I looked at the tiny button of copper in my palm and my eyes watered over. I glanced at Gramps's headstone, then past it to the row of dogwood and elm trees that stood below the cemetery like an army of faithful old friends. Behind the trees, Gregory Bald and Thunderhead Mountain cut into the bright blue sky in two graceful arcs. But they no longer shared a likeness to a couple of bald behinds to me. Nope, they looked more like a pair of angel's wings anchored across the sky. Thin wisps of clouds floated hither and thither at mid-mountain, and for a second I thought that Gramps had simply left one paradise for another.

That ring of mountains around us didn't just keep the new out, it kept the old in. Cades Cove was as perfectly preserved as a pickle. But those old, worn-down mountains weren't as strong as they used to be. They couldn't fight the good fight against airplanes and automobiles and radio signals. They were no match for the chain saw. They couldn't replace the missing panthers, the missing Cherokee, the missing chestnuts . . . the missing Gramps. Nope, Cades Cove was changing. It wasn't going to be a pickle much longer. Unless we did something to keep it crisp and spicy.

I clutched my fist around the penny.

"Colonel Chapman!" I yelled, and raced down the hill as fast as I could to where he was pulling out of the parking area. "Colonel, wait!"

I jumped in front of his auto. The colonel's eyes widened, and Cody gripped the dashboard. The Ford skidded across the gravel and stopped an inch from my kneecaps.

I dashed to the driver's side. "Here!" I said, and shoved the penny at him. "It's a donation for the park. If you promise to keep this place just like it is—no more homes torn down, no more people kicked out—there'll be much more to follow."

Then, almost as an afterthought, I pulled the dynamite from beneath my knickers. "And I believe this belongs to you," I whispered.

I'd meant it as a peace offering, a confession of sorts. But from the look in Colonel Chapman's eyes, being on the receiving end of that stick of dynamite must've seemed like some mighty clever intimidation tactic on my part.

I do things different. It helps to remind yourself of that when you're threatening a government official with a stick of dynamite as you're making a down payment on a national park.

19

I do things different.
It helps to remind
yourself of that
when you realize
that you're an axe
and not a chain saw
after all.

February 7, 1935

Dear Mary Elizabeth, aka Puss,

Thanks for writing! New York City—boy, I had no idea Jeremiah Butler's eggs were world travelers! Next time you write back, send the letter to my new address in Knoxville, Tennessee. My family—well, just my mama and me—moved out of Cades Cove in January to join my pop at long last. Pop works in a textile mill here.

You're dead on—it's a big honor to have our

home made into the Great Smoky Mountains National Park. I won't tell you no tall tales—it hasn't been all shortcake and roses. But Cades Cove is right near heaven, if you ask me. And who doesn't need a little heaven now and again? So I've decided to share.

Most of my neighbors have moved, too. It's been mighty tough, having the friends and family I've known my whole life scattered around like dandelion seeds. Some folks still live in the Cove, though. They pay rent to live there, and once they die, no one will ever live there again.

I've been raising money in my school to help keep Cades Cove as durn near perfect as possible. These are hard times, but the kids bring pennies (and sometimes even nickels!) to class, and we give it to the Park Service. Other schools all around the state started doing it, too, and so far we've collected $1,391.72. If you want to gather pennies at your school, I'd be much obliged. Imagine a New York penny all the way to Cades Cove!

Since I'm not in the Cove anymore, I'm not sure I'd make much of a tour guide. (Though I plan to visit a lot.) My best friend, Cody, still lives there, though, and I know he'd be more than willing to show a redheaded city girl like yourself around. Cody wants to live in the Cove until he's forced to leave, which the park rules say would be when his aunt Matilda kicks. But Aunt Matilda is healthier than a spoonful of castor oil and more stubborn than a nail in hardwood pine. I'm guessing he'll be there till 1983!

Cades Cove isn't a city, like you said in your letter. It's smaller than a bug's ear. But in my heart, it's huge. And it's true there's just one road in and out of Cades Cove. But a clever enough person ought to know: saying there's just one road ain't the same as saying there's just one way to get there.

My best to you and yours (what does that mean, anyways?),

Autumn Winifred Oliver, Knoxville, Tennessee
P.S. Do you like to roller-skate? I'm about the world's best roller skater on wheels.
P.P.S. I'm not a redhead. But I do do things different.

Author's Note

I agree with Autumn: Cades Cove—heck, the whole Great Smoky Mountains National Park!—is right near heaven. Soft, rolling mountains, towering trees, blue-gray wisps of clouds that kiss the tops of both . . . I can just hear Gabriel's horn tooting from atop Mount LaConte!

That's why I decided to tell this story. Because while Autumn Winifred Oliver is a fictional character, the many Cades Cove girls and boys, mothers and fathers, grandmothers and grandfathers were very real. The Great Smoky Mountains National Park is the only national park formed from privately owned land. Hundreds of families gave up the houses and farms they'd lived on their whole lives so the land could become a park. They did so even after they had been told for many years "not to fear"— their land was *not* to be included in the park but would instead border it. These families of eastern Tennessee and western North Carolina decided to share the beauty of their home with everyone in the world. It was not easy, and the families were often not treated fairly. But because of their generosity, the Great Smoky Mountains National Park is now the most-visited national park in the United States. And Cades Cove is the most-visited section of the park.

There was an Oliver family, and it was a prominent one in Cades Cove history. John Oliver was one of the most vocal opponents of the park. Originally, Mr. Oliver supported the idea. Like Gramps, he had dreams of becoming wealthy from tourists flocking to the area. (There really was a sign like the one posted on the fence post in Chapter Six!) But when Cades Cove suddenly became *part of* the park (instead of *next to* it, as was originally planned), he quickly changed his mind and spent the rest of his life—and much of his personal savings—fighting the national park.

And there really was a Colonel David Chapman. I would like to stress that he was not an evil man—far from it. For this story, I tried to see Colonel Chapman as the residents of Cades Cove— specifically, Autumn—might've seen him. Indeed, the fact that Cove people truly despised Colonel Chapman was no secret; in one instance when the colonel was known to be visiting the Cove, this sign greeted his party:

Col. Chapman you and hoast are notfy, let the Cove peopl alone. Get Out. Get Gone. 40 m. limit.

But Colonel Chapman was a man of great civic duty, and his contributions to the Great Smoky Mountains National Park are unparalleled. Without him, there might be no national park. Most likely the land would've fallen into the hands of loggers, and the Cove and its unique culture would've been lost to the teeth of a chain saw. It is unclear from my research exactly how Cades Cove became a part of the park instead of bordering it, but that is not the fault of just one man.

The park founders had enough foresight to realize that once Cades Cove and the surrounding areas became swamped with tourists, the unique lifestyle the residents had developed would quickly disappear. They took painstaking measures to preserve the lifestyle in print. Interviewers toured the region for years, recording the history of the area. They captured *everything*, from the types of clothes the mountain folk wore to the types of games they played. It's a time capsule of sorts, and it's all located in a park library in the Sugarlands Visitor Center near Gatlinburg.

In fact, some of the adventures Autumn undertakes truly did happen to real people. The story of Autumn propping open the mouths of geese with tiny sticks was just too good to make up!

The people of Cades Cove were both superstitious and religious. This is a unique combination of beliefs, and I've tried to capture that fully. I've also tried to accurately depict the geography and cultural flavor of Cades Cove. All of the last names in the text were "borrowed" from Cove history. Any mistakes are fully mine.

And speaking of "mistakes" . . . the time line of this story was compressed to cover the last half of 1934. It actually took many years to form the Great Smoky Mountains National Park. Negotiations for land began as early as 1927, and the official dedication of the park by Franklin Delano Roosevelt didn't occur until September 2, 1940. But he *did* meander through the park and ruffle the hair of the children!

Schoolchildren did raise funds for the park by bringing pennies and nickels to school. The total Autumn mentions in her letter to Puss ($1,391.72) was the money raised in Tennessee alone. Of the schools that participated, the average child donated thirty-one cents. That may not sound like a lot now, but this was during the Great Depression, and thirty-one cents could buy a writing tablet, several pencils, some chewing gum, and some candy!

The people of Cades Cove were fiercely loyal to the government of the United States. During the Civil War, many families in east Tennessee, including most of those in Cades Cove, declared themselves Unionist—a very dangerous thing for them to do in a Confederate state. And yet just seventy-five years later—within the span of one lifetime—the country that they loved so much left them all but homeless, giving them no choice but to forfeit the land they'd always owned.

Cades Cove is a pristine example of pioneer life even today. The families who lived there had the honor of having their land and their lifestyles preserved. The Cove is today just shy of hallowed ground, hosting more than two million visitors each year. You, too, could plan a visit and check out the places where kids like Autumn prayed, slept, and, yes, relieved themselves.

Kristin O'Donnell Tubb

Tina Cahalan Jones

KRISTIN O'DONNELL TUBB
grew up in east Tennessee, near Cades Cove.
"Autumn's story came to me when I was on a guided
tour of Great Smoky Mountains National Park,"
she says. "There we were, standing in what was once
someone's home, and I thought: What if my home
became a national park? How does something like that
even happen? When I did a little research, I discovered
the fascinating history of the people of Cades Cove."
Kristin lives in middle Tennessee with her
husband and two children.